D0113950

PATRIOTS
REDCOATS
& SPIES

American Revolutionary War Adventures

PATRIOTS REDCOATS & SPIES

Robert J. Skead
with Robert A. Skead

ZONDERkidz

ZONDERKIDZ

Patriots, Redcoats and Spies
Copyright © 2015 by Robert J. Skead
Illustrations © 2015 Wilson Ong

This title is also available as a Zondervan ebook.
Visit www.zondervan.com/ebooks.

Requests for information should be addressed to:

Zonderkidz, 3900 *Sparks Drive SE, Grand Rapids, Michigan 49546*

Library of Congress Cataloging-in-Publication Data

Skead, Robert, author.
    Patriots, Redcoats and spies : a Revolutionary War adventure / written by
Robert J. Skead with Robert A. Skead.
        pages cm
    Summary: When Revolutionary War patriot Lamberton Clark is shot by
the British, he enlists the help of his twin fourteen-year-old sons, John and
Ambrose, to get a secret letter to General George Washington.
    ISBN 978-0-310-74841-0 (hardback) — ISBN 978-0-310-74836-6 (epub)
    1. United States—History—Revolution, 1775-1783—Juvenile fiction. [1. United
States—History—Revolution, 1775-1783—Fiction. 2. Spies—Fiction. 3. Brothers—
Fiction. 4. Twins—Fiction. 5. Christian life—Fiction.] I. Skead, Robert A.,
author. II. Title.
PZ7.S62582Pat 2015
[Fic]—dc22   2014031675

Cover design: Deborah Washburn
Cover and interior illustration: Wilson Ong
Interior design and composition: Greg Johnson/Textbook Perfect

Printed in the United States of America

15 16 17 18 19 20 /DCI/ 20 19 18 17 16 15 14 13 12 11 10 9 8 7 6 5 4 3 2

FOR MY FATHER

Thank you for the endless hours of genealogy you spent
proving we are in the Clark family bloodline
and Sons of the American Revolution,
for instilling in me a love for our nation and history—
and for your outstanding creativity with this story.
You never cease to amaze me.
What a joy it is to do this book series with you!

CONTENTS

Chapter 1

Escape From New York

Long Island, New York
July 1777

John Clark didn't know which was worse: that he could barely see where he was going or that his heart was pounding so fast he thought it might pop out of his chest. With trembling hands, he shoved aside the tall reeds as he struggled to maneuver his way through the darkness and the fog. "I should never have listened to you," he gasped to his twin brother as they ran.

Ambrose stumbled over an invisible lump in the ground and nearly fell. "Why is it always my fault?" he panted.

"Because it always is!"

Their father, Lamberton, brought up the rear, gliding soundlessly through the fog. "It's both your faults," he said through clenched teeth. "You will never follow me again. I will see to that."

John glanced back. The darkness hid the look he knew his father gave them. If only he had followed his gut, not listened to his brother, and stayed on the mainland as his father had ordered. Then their lives wouldn't be in danger. They wouldn't be running through the dark, desperately searching for their boat while the enemy closed in.

As if in response to his thoughts, a shot rang out. John dove to the ground. His father and brother landed inches from him as a musket ball cut through the reeds a few feet away.

Too close. Closing his eyes, John tried to still his heaving chest and waited for another shot. Would this be the one that met its mark?

I don't want to die. God, help me. Help us.

Silence. He opened his eyes again to see his father nodding at him. With a deep breath, John bolted to his feet and raced through the tall grass towards the water. His father and brother matched every step.

"Hurry up, brother," came Ambrose's trembling voice. "I'm almost running you over."

"I'm going as fast as I can." Eyes straining, John searched the fog for his father's sailboat. His legs burned as he summoned his last bit of strength and leaped over a small gulley. A film of sweat covered his forehead and body.

Please God, lift this fog, if only for a moment. A soft *splish* rose from his next step. "We're at the water's edge," he hissed. "We're close!"

The three slowed down, their footsteps gently padding along the shore as they searched the mist for the shape of their boat. They were running out of time.

Another shot rang out. It sliced through the grass about two feet to John's left. The two Redcoats were trying their luck. Shooting in the dark.

"They can't run and reload at the same time in this marsh," their father whispered. "That's good."

"Patriot pig! I'll kill you!" shouted a voice behind them. The soldier sounded to be about fifty yards away. Too close.

A second voice followed. "If he doesn't, I will!"

"They think there's only one of us," said Ambrose with a shaky grin.

Their father nodded. "That's why they only sent two men after us ... or me."

"It's the fog." John peeked over his shoulder. No one could be seen. The Redcoats had surely stopped running and were reloading. If they survived, their father's punishment for their impatience and disobedience would surely be severe. John picked up speed again along the rocky shore and then stumbled, throwing out an arm. Ambrose caught and steadied him.

"One lucky shot and one of us is dead or wounded," their father said. "You boys stay in front of me. And stay low." His voice was tense. John felt sick to his stomach. How could he have gotten them into this mess?

The three continued along the shoreline, picking their way around rocks and weeds. Suddenly, a white light pierced the mist from above. *Thank God.* John glanced up at the half moon and scanned the shoreline ahead for their sixteen-foot skiff. It lay anchored somewhere close by, he was sure of it. He just couldn't see it. He rounded a gentle curve in the shoreline, and then there it was — their boat, rocking gently on the waves about thirty feet away.

They entered the water, forcing themselves to slide slowly so they didn't splash. Seconds later, thick clouds hid the moon again.

Ambrose grabbed the rope attached to the anchor near the bow of the boat and gently pulled it up while Lamberton placed his left leg over the side of the boat and rolled himself inside. Ambrose dropped the anchor inside the hull as John heaved himself into the craft, followed a moment later by his brother. The two of them crouched against the hull of the boat and ducked their heads.

"Guess we'll have to come back another day for the rowboat we borrowed," John whispered, locking eyes with his brother.

Lamberton had already begun to raise the sail. As he hauled on the line, the craft turned into the wind.

"There he is!" a voice echoed over the water. John peeked over the edge of the boat and spotted two Redcoats emerging from the reeds on the shore, guns raised.

The wind howled fiercely as waves rocked the boat in the Long Island Sound, but it caught the sail and sent them speeding into open water. John caught one last glimpse of the Redcoats before they faded through the fog. Just then,

another shot exploded in the air, and his father jerked and grunted. John turned to see red blooming on Lamberton's back. The musket ball had ripped through the flesh above his right shoulder blade.

"Dad!" John's voice caught in his throat.

His father fell to his knees as a second shot whizzed by and plunked into the water. The wind was blowing away the fog, allowing the soldiers better aim. John looked at his brother. Did his own face look as frightened as his twin's?

"Ambrose, get us out of here." Lamberton sat down heavily in the bottom of the boat near John and motioned his hand toward the other side of the bay. Seconds later, he fell back with a groan, thumping into John's arms. John struggled to support the sudden weight.

With a gasp, Ambrose lurched up and tied off the sail, then grabbed control of the tiller. Ducking back down, he steered the boat away from the shore toward Connecticut.

Behind them, the sounds of cursing carried across the water.

As the skiff skipped rapidly over the waves, John braced his legs against the floor and pushed his father's shoulder away so he could inspect his back. Blood soaked through the shirt. John knew he had to stop the bleeding. But how?

Settling his father gently on his stomach, John frantically searched the hull for a rag. He found one tucked under an old buoy and placed it over his father's wound. His hands were trembling. "Are you all right?"

No response. John's heart skipped a beat.

"Dad?" Ambrose's voice shook even as he smoothly navigated them away from danger. He was sitting a few feet away, gripping the tiller with white knuckles.

"I'll be all right," their father said, his voice little louder than a whisper. After a pause, he tried to roll over and sit up.

"Are you sure that's a good idea, Dad?" John asked as he slowly guided his father back into a sitting position. "Don't you want to lie down?" A beam of moonlight reflected off John's blood-soaked hand. Ambrose shuddered.

Their father reached over his shoulder and covered John's hand, putting pressure on his wound. "I'm all right," their father said again, though his voice was still shaky. "I don't think it hit anything vital." He took a shallow breath.

"We'll get you to a doctor," said John. Salty water sprayed in his face as the boat bounced over a wave. He wiped his eyes on his sleeve.

Their father closed his eyes and leaned his shoulder against the side of the boat. He winced as it hit a wave and he thudded against the side. "Steer us to where I left you boys yesterday, Ambrose — where you were supposed to be waiting for me." He opened his eyes and looked pointedly at each of them. Even through the pain clearly written on his face, John could see his disapproval. "Fourteen-year-olds should know enough to obey their father."

Ambrose pounded the side of the hull. "If you'd come back when you said you would, we would have stayed where we were." His tone was both surly and guilty. "I felt we had to do it."

John glared at him before turning back to their father. "We never should have left to find you. I'm sorry." He adjusted the rag and pressed harder on the wound. His fingertips were already slick with blood, and John fought back a wave of nausea. "But why were those men chasing us? What did you do? And why'd you have us slit those sails?" A wave bounced him in his seat, and his father breathed in sharply. "Dad?"

His father's face was twisted in pain, and for a moment he said nothing. "Thank Providence for the fog and that they didn't see you with me," he said at last. He paused and gingerly reached back to touch the rag John still held. "But I wish I could see the look on their faces when they discover the slashed sails."

Not for the first time that night, John thought back through the events of the last hours. When their father had asked John and Ambrose to wait for him on the opposite side of the sound, he told them that he'd be back in several hours. He was just going to visit with a friend in New York to talk about making some new masts for him. He never mentioned he was going to check out the British ships to make sure they weren't preparing for an attack on Connecticut or that he had arranged some sort of secret meeting. When he took too long to return, the boys worried and went to find him. The next thing they knew, they were helping him cut British sails and running for their lives.

"It'll be some time before they're seaworthy again," said Ambrose. "As a seaman, I didn't enjoy destroying them."

"It will take a bigger effort to launch one of their larger ships to come after me," Lamberton replied. He winced as John removed the rag and then quickly replaced it with more pressure. The wound was still bleeding heavily. "They'll do it," Lamberton said through gritted teeth. "But it will take at least an hour. Maybe two."

"Why are they after you?" John asked. He shielded his eyes from another wash of spray as the skiff sliced through the water.

With a grimace, Lamberton reached for his left breast pocket, hissing as he carefully pulled out a leather case. "Because of this. Or rather what's inside it."

John struggled to steady his voice. "What's inside it?"

"A very special letter."

Ambrose looked over his shoulder from where he steered and leaned in to get a better look. "To whom?" he asked. "Or from whom?"

Lamberton held the case over his heart.

"What are you going to do with it?" John peered at the case. There was nothing particularly unusual about it. It had a single flap with a metal buckle, and the leather had been worn smooth in spots from use.

Lamberton looked out at the dark waters of the bay. He shifted his weight, winced, and turned back to Ambrose and John. Finally, he spoke, his voice soft. "I hoped it wouldn't come to this."

John held his breath. What was he talking about?

Lamberton cleared his throat. When he continued,

17

his voice was louder. "What's in this case is extremely important."

"What's inside?" John asked. He glanced at the leather case his father still held to his chest.

"A message to George Washington. I don't know what it says, but I know the contents are extremely time sensitive." He paused. "It's from a man we call Culper. The message is in invisible ink." Lamberton bit his lower lip and closed his eyes. "I'm supposed to deliver it. But I'm afraid now I can't finish my mission."

"You're ... a spy?" John asked. John and Ambrose exchanged an incredulous look.

Their father adjusted his position. "I guess you could say that," he breathed. "I prefer the term *patriot*." Suddenly, the skiff hit a large wave and Lamberton's back slammed against John's knee. Lamberton inhaled sharply.

Placing his free hand on his father's shoulder, John said, "We'll get you to a doctor." He hoped he sounded calmer than he felt.

"Then you can finish your mission," Ambrose added. He pointed the craft's tiller toward the dark Fairfield, Connecticut, shore, his brown hair fluttering in the wind. "After you get that ball removed and heal that shoulder."

Lamberton shook his head. His breathing was growing shallower, and even in the dim moonlight John could see that his father's face was pale. He had lost a lot of blood.

"Right, Dad?" John asked. He didn't like seeing his father look so weak. His father was never weak.

"I'm afraid there's no time for that." Lamberton looked at each of his sons in turn, sweat gleaming on his forehead. "That letter needs to get to Washington as soon as possible, and I'm in no condition to deliver it."

A gust of wind jolted the boat, and John had to grip the side to keep from bouncing out. "Can't someone else take it?"

Lamberton shook his head. His voice had grown very faint, and John had to lean in to hear him above the waves. "I've been compromised," he whispered.

"What?" John stared back. "By someone you know?"

"Could be. Maybe someone in Connecticut or New York. We may never know." An extreme weariness came into his father's eyes, but whether it was from the bullet wound or something else, John wasn't sure. "Those Redcoats shouldn't have been so close behind me." Lamberton paused to catch his breath. "The truth is I don't know whom I can trust." He eyed them intently. "I had hoped this wouldn't be the case, but ... Now, I only have two hopes for getting this secret message to George Washington." Lamberton took a shallow breath. "And I'm looking at them."

CHAPTER 2

DOUBLE TROUBLE

U s?" John threw a frantic look at Ambrose. His father couldn't mean that they should become spies. He was injured. He had lost a lot of blood. Clearly he wasn't thinking straight.

"We'll do it," Ambrose said immediately, nodding. He obviously didn't have the same reservations.

"We'll what?" John demanded. "You can't be serious. Us? Spies? We only turned fourteen last month."

"Not spies," his father said. "Patriots." He paused and his brown eyes, normally so stern and hard, looked at John gently. John looked away. "You're the only two people I can trust. And there's no time to find anyone else."

John watched his father's head bob and eyes grow weary.

"As couriers," Lamberton panted, "your youth will help you not to be stopped and questioned."

"But, Dad." John felt on the verge of panic.

"I'm sorry to ask this of you, John." His father's voice was a whisper. "You'll be safer together. The two of you, like it's always been. Nathan Hale was only twenty when he joined the Cause. And I ..." He shifted and groaned slightly. "I can't do it myself." He sighed deeply. "I'm exhausted," he whispered. A few moments later, John felt his father's body go limp in his arms. He had either fallen asleep or passed out — John wasn't sure.

"Ambrose, get us to shore fast!" John cried, his voice catching in his throat.

Ambrose aimed the tiller so the skiff avoided a large wave. "I'm doing the best I can! I can't believe you don't want to help him."

John looked up at his brother. "I do want to help — help him get to a doctor."

John gazed into the darkness of the early morning hours. If only he were more like his father. He'd wait until they arrived on shore and somehow talk his dad into finding someone else.

▲ ▲ ▲

Finally, an hour later, beams of golden light began to bathe the clouds in the east. As the Clark-family skiff sliced through the chop of the Long Island Sound, John's eyes remained riveted on the Connecticut shore. How could he convince his father to find another person to carry the letter? He knew that his father's identity had been compromised, but surely there was someone — someone — that his father trusted. John pursed his lips and glanced at the bloody rag on his father's back. He was worried about how much blood his father had lost. It couldn't be good. In the soft light, John could see how pale and clammy his face was. John's eyes shifted to the precious case his father clutched against his chest. What was in the letter it contained? Something that could change the course of the war? His father said it had to get to General Washington fast.

Was it really going to be up to him and Ambrose to make that happen?

As a familiar bend in the shoreline swung into view, Ambrose called out. "There's the spot!" He aimed the craft toward the beach. John looked down as their father stirred. His eyes cracked open, but he made no move to sit up.

The vessel hit the sandy shore with a jolt. The brothers jumped into the water, and John planted his feet firmly into the sand to keep his balance while he and Ambrose tugged the boat as far onto the shore as possible. John helped his father out of the boat and onto the dry sand. Ambrose quickly wrapped the sail around the mast, tied a sailor's knot to secure it, and lowered it out of view.

Lamberton took a few unsteady steps and fell to his knees, then rested there as John knelt at his side. Ambrose flanked him on the other side.

"I'll be all right." Their father waved them away. "Don't worry." He grunted in pain as he checked his wound. The bleeding had stopped. With a breath, his father lifted his hand and rested it on John's neck. "I appreciate the help." He looked at him intently before shifting his gaze to Ambrose. "Now listen . . . there isn't much time. It won't be long before those Lobsterbacks search the coastline for me. You two have to finish what I've begun —"

"We've got to get you to a doctor," John insisted. "We can't leave you like this."

"No." John was startled by the sudden strength in his father's voice. It left no room for argument.

"But Dad —"

"No! Listen to me and memorize every word I tell you. You boys are Sons of Liberty. Just like me. You're expert marksmen. I've taught you everything I know." He paused, his voice softening. "You're the only ones I can trust. It could be someone I know who's telling the British of my actions." Lamberton swayed slightly, and for a moment John wondered if his father was going to faint. "I didn't think I'd need you to do this, but in life and in war, we must always be prepared. I had hoped I'd be sending you back home right now —" He reached into his pocket and took out the leather case again — the case that contained the letter to General Washington. "Guard this with your lives. Stay together no matter what happens. You both have to get this to General George Washington in New Jersey. If you travel quickly, you should be able to connect with him somewhere near Morristown. It should only take you a few days to get there. You boys are clever. Use your wits and find him."

"We will, Dad," Ambrose said.

"Can't we get you to a doctor first?" John implored. "Please, Dad?" A gentle wind blew sand against his feet and legs.

"No. There's no time for that. I was told that this letter is of the utmost importance. Vital news for Washington. You have to help your country first. Now is your time." Lamberton waved the boys in closer. "Take this to the General. Remember. Tell him it's from Culper Junior. The message is in invisible ink. You got that?"

"But —" John started to speak again, only to be cut off by his father's upraised hand.

"Trust no one," added Lamberton. "Those loyal to the king pose as patriots. They can and will deceive you, and if caught, you'll either be handed over as traitors or ..." He braced himself. "Or killed on the spot as such. Both sides have spies everywhere."

"Like you?" Ambrose said proudly. He had obviously ignored the "killed" comment that was making John sick to his stomach.

"Like *us*," their father replied. He grunted in pain, and held out the leather case.

John stared at it. He glanced at his brother, whose face grew serious, then reached for the case. It was rough and sturdy.

Ambrose assured his father. "We'll be careful. No one will be trusted. We're just a couple of kids traveling to see some relatives."

"That's right." Lamberton let out a slight moan as he rose to his feet. He stood firmly for a moment, then started to sink back to his knees. Ambrose's arms quickly came to his aid. John placed his right arm around his father's waist.

Flanked by both his sons, Lamberton said, "Don't worry about me. I'll find help. You just go." He took a shaky step forward. "And whatever you do … don't get caught."

John exhaled. They hanged spies. Like Nathan Hale.

His father must have read his mind. He looked at John, then Ambrose, squarely in the eye. "I would never ask you to do this if I didn't think there was any other way." For a second, tears seemed to fill their father's eyes, but they were gone before John could be sure he had really seen them. "I'm proud of you." The brothers reached the grass and released their father. They stood by his side for a moment, making sure he could stand.

John dreaded this final goodbye. "How will we know who the general is?" he stalled.

"He'll be the tallest one," said Lamberton. "He stands at six foot three."

"He'll also be the one they call general, big brother," Ambrose said.

Lamberton nodded and steadied himself on the trunk of a tree. "Every message to Washington must be delivered as quickly as possible. This is a war of information and wits." Their father turned to John. "You have my musket?"

"Yes, we left it over there, hidden with the other one."

"Good. You know what's special about mine, right?"

John nodded.

"Good. Now go. And go fast. Mind every word I said. Stay together and trust no one."

"Okay," said John. He didn't trust himself to say more.

Uncharacteristically, Ambrose leaned in to his father's side. He spoke almost formally. "We'll find General Washington. Don't worry. You have my word." He grabbed his father's good shoulder. "I love you, Father."

Their father smiled at him in return. He gave the same smile to John. "How many times do I have to tell you? Go!"

The brothers turned and sprinted toward the campsite where they had been waiting for their father the day before. As they ran, John glanced at the Long Island Sound. Sails had appeared on the horizon. British sails. His father was right. The Redcoats would be searching everywhere.

Father is always right.

Moments later, John and Ambrose reached their camp. John quickly knelt down, opened his satchel, and carefully secured the case containing the letter. "I hope the words in that letter really are important enough for us to risk our lives," he said.

"Dad says they are and that's good enough for me." Ambrose picked up their blankets and the muskets they had hidden in the brush earlier.

John eyed his brother. "It's good enough for me too. I was just—"

"We better move fast."

Frustrated, John fastened his satchel. Did Ambrose

think him too weak, too easily frightened? "Yes. We have a lot to figure out and a lot of territory to cover."

"I wish we had our muskets when those Redcoats were shooting at us," said Ambrose.

"I wasn't going to risk ruining or losing our weapons in that rinky-dink rowboat you suggested we borrow," John snapped. "And we do have to get that boat back."

"We'll get it back," Ambrose said. "Later."

I hope so. But when? John had had every intention of returning the rowboat when they decided to use it. It pained him to think that by not returning it, they'd essentially stolen it.

Maybe someone else will find it and return it to its owner.

John gave the campsite a final perusal to make sure they had everything. This wouldn't be their last time in Fairfield, would it? John hoped not. A lump formed in his throat. "Let's go, Ambrose."

"Yes, let's go."

As Ambrose took hold of his satchel, his face suddenly lit up. He reached inside his bag and pulled out his fife. Before John knew it, Ambrose was running back in the direction of their father with his fife in hand. He disappeared around the bend and returned a few minutes later, empty-handed.

"I gave it to Dad," Ambrose said. "Just in case he needs to make a loud noise or call for help."

"Good idea," John said, knowing his brother had given his father one of his most prized possessions. "Now, let's go."

▲ ▲ ▲

The woods along the Connecticut shoreline lay thick with trees — mostly pine and some oak. John and Ambrose scurried along a narrow path, jumping over fallen logs and large rocks and dodging low-hanging branches.

Fighting an urge to yawn, John pushed his body to continue. He knew they needed to get far from the shoreline before the Redcoats landed and began their search, but he was exhausted from lack of sleep. They would need a map to find the fastest route to Morristown. Someone would have to give them directions. John's thoughts turned to his father where they had left him on the shore. Would he find help? What if the bleeding started again? What if a loyalist found him? Or the Redcoats? John kept jogging, one foot in front of the other. He wouldn't think about it.

Instead John watched his brother. The twins were identical, but only in looks. Anyone who knew them could tell the difference as soon as one of them opened his mouth. The Clark boys shared the same straight brown hair, the same noble nose and firm jawline. They had the same laugh. But in matters of humor and will they were as different as they could be. John knew Ambrose considered this trip an adventure. John himself was terrified.

"What do you think's in that letter?" Ambrose said suddenly, examining the position of the rising sun.

"Who knows? But Dad got shot for it, so it's not some stupid love letter, that's for sure."

"I can't believe Dad's a spy," Ambrose said as he leapt up and off a rock.

How did he have so much energy? "Bet he's the best one they have," said John.

Ambrose nodded. "Agreed."

John gave his brother a startled look. At least there was one thing they could agree upon.

After about an hour, the shade of the woods disappeared as the trees thinned and they came to a field and farm. The brothers stared momentarily at the fork in the path. To the right was the way home. The way their father would follow — if he could make it that far. To the left, a small village and ultimately the route to New Jersey. Looking down the road that led home, John paused, then went that way.

"What are you doing?" Ambrose demanded.

"Going home to get help. We can use our horses," said John. "Or better yet, maybe Enoch or Samuel can do this for us," he said, naming two of their older brothers. Deep inside, he knew only Berty could possibly have the skills to do it, but he was with the militia and not at home.

Ambrose bolted forward and stood in front of his brother. "We can't do that! We live too far away. We'd lose time by going all the way there and back. Dad said it had to be us. Our age is on the mission's side. Mom would never let us — or them — go. If that was an option, Dad would have suggested it."

"I don't care. I'm going." John took a step to the left.

Ambrose pushed his brother in the chest. "No, you're

not. Dad said *we* have to hurry and deliver that letter. If you don't want to do it, then give me the letter. I'll go alone."

John snorted. "Yeah, like I'm going to let that happen."

Ambrose crossed his arms. "I could do it without you."

"You'd get yourself killed."

"I can do it. Give me the letter." Ambrose held out his hand.

John shook his head. "I listened to you before, and we ended up messing up Dad's mission and almost getting killed."

"But this is not about listening to me," said Ambrose. "It's about obeying Dad."

John opened his mouth to retort — then closed it again. Narrowing his eyes, he considered all the options, all the possibilities. There was no escaping it — as much as he hated to admit it, his twin was right. They'd already gotten into this mess by disobeying their father once. They couldn't do it again.

With a huff, John looked at Ambrose and frowned. "All right. We'll go that way." With a last glance at the safety of home, he turned on his heels and pushed past his brother and down the path toward New Jersey.

CHAPTER 3

FURIOUS LOBSTERBACKS

Sergeant Conrad Evans stood at the bow of the British ship and peered through his spyglass. His greasy black hair barely moved in the wind. Under his left eye he proudly wore a thick white scar, remnants from a bayonet fight with an American colonist who hadn't lived to tell the tale of their encounter.

He was hoping to see, somewhere, the small skiff floating aimlessly in the tide with a dead traitor inside. As his ship closed in on the Connecticut coast, his face reddened with anger. Evans had been given secret information about the colonist and his actions, but the man was crafty and had eluded him several times, damaged three of his Navy's vessels, and gotten away — again — with important information. It was more than an embarrassment. Evans knew his shot had connected with the traitor spy — he had heard him grunt. He had only hoped it was close enough to a vital organ to cause his death. If dead, he or some local loyalist would find him, he hoped.

Evans' commanding officer, Lieutenant Williams, stood beside him on the deck. "You must find that traitor and intercept that letter," Williams said, interrupting his thoughts. Evans put down the spyglass. Williams' black scarf and hair fluttered in the wind. "There will be a promotion in it for you both if you succeed."

Williams addressed both Evans and Corporal Carl Sheffield who stood to Evans' left. The corporal was a round yet powerful man with bushy brows and thin lips. Williams paused, then said, "I also want you to *kill* this traitor-courier and any others you discover who are involved with their efforts. We'll send a message loud and clear to these rebels that we are *dead* serious about spies. We will take no prisoners." The commander glared at Evans and Sheffield, ensuring his order was received. When he saw the determined look in their eyes, he turned on his heels and left.

"Wounded animals always leave a trail," growled Evans to Corporal Sheffield beside him. "I will find this spy, if he still lives, and he will hang from the gallows for many to see."

As the ship cut through the bay, Evans raised his spyglass again and examined the edge of the shoreline. Moments later, he saw a skiff nestled safely ashore. Was it the spy's? There was only one way to find out. Evans whistled loudly, turned his head, and locked eyes with the ship's captain. He pointed to the boat on the beach.

The captain gave an order. A small sail was sent down, and with a turn of the rudder, the vessel aimed right toward the shore where the Clarks had landed that morning.

As a spray of salt water splashed Sergeant Evans in the face, he took off his red coat and tossed it aside. "This hunt," he said to Sheffield, "will require more covert measures."

Sheffield nodded and the two of them watched the approaching shore in silence for a few minutes before going below to gather supplies.

"I wonder the name of this spy and if he still breathes," Evans muttered as they returned to their position on the deck, knapsacks in hand. "I will make an example of this elusive pig."

Sheffield smiled at his sergeant, revealing a mouth of crooked yellow teeth. "Forget the gallows. If he's still breathing, it won't be for long." He placed a hand on his pistol. Its short silver barrel glistened in the morning light.

CHAPTER 4

IT MUST BE FUN TO BE A TWIN

A church bell rang in the distance. John wiped beads of sweat from his forehead. He was hot all over. Even his feet felt hot. He brushed damp sand off his trousers as he walked. How in the world were they going to get all the way to New Jersey when he was struggling to survive a few hours down the road?

Trust Providence. That's what their Dad would say.

"We'll need horses." Ambrose adjusted his shoulder bag. A patch of sweat had formed under the strap, soaking his shirt. "Keep your eye out."

John froze in his tracks. "They hang horse thieves too, right?"

"If they get caught," Ambrose said mischievously.

"Great." John kicked the ground and started walking again. "Now we'll have two reasons I can have a noose around my neck." He picked up his pace to a jog.

Ambrose matched his speed.

A dead sparrow lay on the dirt road, and John zigzagged to jump over it. His satchel and sleeping pad thumped against his body rhythmically, and he breathed deeply as he ran. The smell of the ocean was replaced by the stench of cow manure from a pasture nearby. John rubbed his nose. "You stink."

"No. Sorry. That's you," Ambrose replied, switching his musket to his other arm as he ran ahead of his brother.

John shook his head, dashed in front of Ambrose, and jumped over a hole in the road. Moments later, Ambrose was at his side again.

So he wants to race. John pumped his legs harder. "Running with a musket and all this stuff isn't easy," he said. He looked over. Ambrose was still beside him.

"Who's making up excuses now?" Ambrose kept pace. He stutter-stepped over a pile of horse dung.

John's side cramped as he ran faster. The July sun burned the morning dew off their surroundings and beat upon their faces. Ambrose pulled ahead, and John glared at his brother's back. The race was ridiculous. They were burning energy they needed to conserve. Ambrose was cocky, reckless, always jumping into things without thinking. John was going to have to watch him closely so they didn't take any unnecessary risks. *We're just two boys visiting relatives. If we don't look suspicious or do something stupid we can do this. I hope.*

John slowed his pace. "You win! There. You feel better

about yourself?" He stopped and bent over with his hands on his knees.

"Yes. Yes, I do feel better." Ambrose turned and, breathing hard, walked back to his brother.

John wiped the sweat from his forehead and opened his canteen. He took a deep drink. The water lifted his spirits even though it had already grown lukewarm. He handed Ambrose the canteen. "It doesn't matter, Ambrose. So you're faster than me. Big deal."

"I'm also a better knife thrower."

John waved off his brother. "Who cares about your silly tricks? I always win at the things that count. Like Sophie."

At the mention of the young woman whose attention they'd been fighting over the past few months, Ambrose's eyes narrowed. Then he laughed. "You wish! It's good to have dreams. Just not too lofty. Sophie's my girl, and when she finds out I delivered an important message to George Washington, she'll be even more impressed with me." Ambrose thumped his chest.

"I have the letter, remember?" John patted his satchel. "This isn't about you. Information that could affect the course of the war could be in that case."

"True," reflected Ambrose. "Maybe it's better if I hold it."

"Yeah, right." John rolled his eyes. "The fate of the country in your hands." He grimaced and returned his canteen to his bag before continuing to walk. Who was he kidding? The letter wasn't even secure in *his* hands. Why did his father have to join this war? Why did John have to be involved?

He could be home now ... building his boat or walking with Sophie. He smiled as he pictured her strawberry-blonde hair bouncing off her shoulders as she rode her horse on his family's property. It would be him she'd be proud of. He was the one she left special notes for after all. Yes. He'd do the right thing, like he always tried to do. Just like Dad. And he'd look after Ambrose and that letter. Surely, God wouldn't let anything bad happen to them. Maybe he could become a committed patriot and live to enjoy independence.

Or maybe not. Maybe he'd end up dead like Nathan Hale. So many families were being broken up by this war. Hopefully his wouldn't be one of them.

John's pulse quickened. To think a few days ago he'd actually told Ambrose he was bored. That wouldn't be an issue now.

But was the cause of liberty truly worth risking one's life for? He had figured he'd have more time to wrestle with that question when he was old enough to enlist. His mother had cried all day when she learned about Berty's enlistment. She would cry an ocean when she found out about the mission their father had sent them on.

Ambrose seemed to be thinking similar thoughts. "I thought it would be a few years before we got involved in the war," he said. "But here we are. This is exciting."

John lifted his pack slightly to get some fresh air on his sweaty back. "I hoped it would be over by the time we had to decide. I'm only doing this to help Dad. Honestly, I don't know why Berty and the neighbors enlisted."

Ambrose stopped in his tracks. "Are you crazy? If Dad heard you talk like that, he'd — "

"Dad respects my opinions, ok?" Suddenly angry, John stopped in the middle of the road and grabbed his brother's shirt. "I can think what I like, Ambrose."

Ambrose put his sweaty hands on John's fist and pushed it off his shirt. "Fine." He stomped ahead.

John's mind shifted back to their task at hand. "To make sure we don't risk our lives, we do as Dad says and trust no one." John raised his voice as he caught up to his brother.

Ambrose lifted his hand. "Except the guys in the militia. We can trust them. They're Sons of Liberty. Committed to winning freedom, brother, like I thought you were." He narrowed his eyes at John.

"I'm just following Dad's orders. That's all I'm committed to right now. You're the patriot. Maybe we can trust guys in the militia. Maybe not. In this case, we do as Dad says — trust no one." John shifted his musket onto his other shoulder.

Ambrose hesitated. "Agreed. We're not home. We have no way of knowing who's loyal to the King of England and who's a patriot."

The boys continued trekking along the road. Soon a cluster of wooden buildings came into view. "We've been here before," said John, recognizing the blacksmith shop and general store.

Ambrose nodded. "That was several years ago."

The morning brought all sorts of activity to the streets.

As they approached, a man with a tired, pale face swept the front stoop of his pottery shop. A plump woman with black, prickly hair that stuck out of a white cap poured water into a bowl for a dog, who quickly lapped it up and lay down by the front door.

As they turned the corner in front of a dry goods shop, several young men appeared dressed in black socks, black knickers, and loose white shirts. All wore black tri-corn hats.

"Must be members of the Connecticut Militia," Ambrose whispered to John.

John nodded. "Probably guarding the coast from potential British invasion."

Ambrose's face lit up. He tugged on John's sleeve. "Militiamen mean horses must be nearby."

"You're right. Good thinking." John slapped his brother on the back. "But first — directions." He spotted a young soldier across the street. "Excuse me!" he called.

The soldier, who had stopped to pet the shopkeeper's dog, looked up. He looked to be about twenty.

John walked up to him. "We need to get to Morristown, New Jersey. Can you point out the best road to get there?"

The soldier smiled as he glanced at John and Ambrose. "Anyone ever tell you, you two look alike?"

John rolled his eyes and knew his twin was doing the same. "We're twins," John replied shortly.

"But which one of us looks more like the other?" joked Ambrose, waving his hand between himself and his brother.

The soldier froze and wrinkled his brow while he thought. He ran a skinny hand through his sweaty black hair.

Ambrose cracked a smile at John, who clenched his fists. He didn't think now was the best time for jokes. "Which way to New Jersey?" John repeated.

The soldier paused and studied the twins. "Are you patriots?"

Ambrose leaned in closer. "Of course we are," he said softly.

John looked at Ambrose. Whatever happened to trusting no one? But maybe Ambrose was right to admit their loyalty so quickly. This side of the North River, it would only arouse suspicion if they lied or refused to answer. Anyway, the militia was on their side, and this young man didn't look like a spy.

The soldier seemed to notice the hesitation in John's face. "Not to worry," he said and patted John's shoulder. "You're in good company. I only know Hackensack, New Jersey. But, come on." He started walking, and the boys followed. "I'll draw you a map."

The three approached a nearby tavern. Outside it, a poster read:

TO ALL BRAVE, HEALTHY, ABLE BODIED, AND
WELL DISPOSED YOUNG MEN, IN THE NEIGHBOURHOOD,
WHO HAVE ANY INCLINATION TO JOIN THE TROOPS,
NOW RAISING UNDER GENERAL WASHINGTON,
FOR THE DEFENCE OF THE LIBERTIES AND INDEPENDENCE
OF THE UNITED STATES...
TAKE NOTICE.

" 'Well-disposed young men'? That leaves you out, little brother." John poked Ambrose as he opened the door to the tavern.

"At least I'm able-bodied." Ambrose bent his arm and flexed his muscle.

Now it was the soldier's turn to roll his eyes. He shook his head. "You still interested in that map?"

"Yes," the twins said simultaneously.

"Then come on." The soldier went through the door and entered the tavern.

Inside, John carefully opened his satchel and handed a piece of paper to the young man. Wooden tables and chairs were placed throughout the open room, but they were mostly unoccupied. The three of them sat down at an empty table near the counter.

"What are your names?" the soldier asked.

John looked at his twin. *Should we answer?* It was one thing to admit they were Patriots but —

"Gideon," Ambrose stated.

"I'm ... Theophilus," John added.

"I'm Joshua. Private Joshua Carpenter." He turned to the proprietor who stood behind the counter. "May I borrow a quill and some ink?"

Ambrose stared at John, then smiled. "My brother Theophilus here got his name because he was 'the awfullest' baby ... crying all the time."

John kicked Ambrose under the table. "Actually that

was him. Mom simply got us confused when naming us. Us being identical and all."

The proprietor brought Joshua paper, a quill, and ink, and looked back and forth quickly at the twins.

Ambrose shook his head solemnly. "Trust me Joshua, it was him. He's the awfullest singer too."

"Ok, well—" Joshua ignored their bantering and began to sketch out a rough map. "You'll need to cut over this way and take the Kings Ferry to New York."

"Is it safe for us to go on it?" asked Ambrose. "It's important we get to New Jersey fast. Are you sure that's the best way?"

Joshua cocked his head and looked at the brothers suspiciously.

John elbowed Ambrose. "We're just excited to visit family there." He smiled innocently.

Joshua nodded. "It's safe, although it's always a target for the British. But it's controlled by patriots and the only way across the North River without a ship. I'll mark the ferry with an X. Then you head this way to New Jersey. Here's Hackensack. I think there's a road up this way that's often used by the army and goes to Morristown. Maybe you'll meet someone who can help." He chuckled. "Just hope it doesn't rain—the roads get pretty sloppy."

Joshua scratched his matted mass of hair and looked at the boys. "You may run into a closed road. We just got word that a large New Jersey militia is on the move with the general and the Continental troops. There are fifteen thousand Redcoats in New York."

"I hate Lobsterbacks," Ambrose said. "I've heard my father say some not so nice things about that British general."

"Yeah, Cornwallis," Joshua leaned in closer to the boys. "You should hear what our commanding officer says. We're in a difficult situation. Cornwallis and his men could go up the North River and through Lake George. Then he could head to Lake Champlain and on up to Canada."

"So?" said John.

Joshua looked at John quizzically. "That would cut our New England colonies off from the union."

Ambrose gave his brother an exasperated look. "That could mean victory ... for them."

Joshua folded the map and handed it to John. "The Brits could also attack Philadelphia," Joshua said. "They could move on to the southern colonies, too." He huffed. "I'd hate to be General Washington now. There are so many options to consider."

"How long do you think he'll stay in New Jersey?" John was suddenly nervous. He hadn't considered the idea that General Washington would leave the state before he and Ambrose had time to deliver the letter.

Joshua shrugged. "Hard to say. But in New Jersey he has the chance to move to defend any of these places. So I guess it depends on when Cornwallis makes his move."

John looked at Ambrose, but if his brother was worried by this news, he didn't show it.

The smell of baking bread drifted from the back room. A long time had passed since John or his brother had eaten. "I'm starving," said John. As Joshua turned to the proprietor, Ambrose whispered to John, "I bet Washington's moving through New Jersey with our troops to protect the Hudson Valley. Bet the letter details the Redcoats' plans."

Nodding to his brother, John gazed at the map before him. The information they carried could help General Washington makes the right decision. They needed to move fast.

Joshua called to the tavern keeper. "We'd like some bread please, for me and my two new identical friends here."

"But we don't have any money," John protested.

Joshua made a sweeping gesture with his arm. "My treat. You don't meet twins around here every day. You know, you two are the first identical twins I've ever seen. There were twins in my school as a lad, but they were a boy and a girl and not very near in features."

"Good thing for the boy," said Ambrose.

Joshua laughed at John's groan. "Must be fun to be a twin."

"Not really," said John and Ambrose together.

The tavern keeper returned with a small loaf of bread, some jam, and a jug of water for the three of them. Once they had finished eating, Joshua paid the owner and they exited the shop, blinking in the bright sunlight.

John extended his hand to Joshua. "Thank you for your help and for the food."

Joshua nodded. "Good luck. I hope you find your way."
He smiled and headed off down the street.

John glanced at the TAKE NOTICE recruitment poster.
He turned to Ambrose. "So, Gideon, my able-bodied
brother, how are we going to steal the horses?"

Ambrose snorted. "Theophilus? Where'd you get that
name?"

"The Bible." John shrugged. "It was the first thing that
came to me."

CHAPTER 5

THIEVES & ENTERTAINERS

The small corral behind the blacksmith's shop at the edge of town contained twenty horses of various sizes, most about twelve-hands tall. John climbed up on the fence and examined them. Ambrose sat on the top rail beside him.

One brown gelding went nose to nose with a white horse. After a few moments, the white one rose slightly on its hind legs and gave the brown horse a right hook with its hoof. The brown horse darted away.

John laughed quietly. "That's the one I want," he said in a low voice.

"Figures you'd take the bully," Ambrose replied.

"No, I meant the brown one."

Ambrose looked at John with laughter in his eyes. "You'd rather have the loser than the big, mean one? Too bad there're no ponies in there."

John clenched his teeth and ignored him.

Ambrose nudged his brother. "I like that black and white one there," he whispered. "The one with all the mares around him."

"That figures. No. That horse is nasty. I can tell. Trust me. I'll get the perfect horse for you." John nudged his brother. "But let's get out of here. We look too conspicuous."

Ambrose laughed. He jumped off the fence and together they headed back toward town.

Once they were far enough from the corral, John said, "I feel bad about this."

"Me too." Ambrose turned to look back at the horses. "Mom will kill us if she ever finds out."

"And if anyone else finds out … we'll be hanged." John pointed left. "But there's the road to New York." He pointed back. "And there are the horses. We have no choice."

John and Ambrose hid their muskets and gear behind a large oak tree near the main road across the street from the stable, and John shared the plan he'd come up with. He put a hand on his brother's shoulder. "You just do what you're supposed to do and I'll do my job. We'll meet at the designated place and go from there to find George Washington."

Ambrose grinned. "Don't forget to steal me a nice comfortable saddle too."

"Yes, the prince must always be comfortable." John faked a bow.

Leaving his brother, John ran through town and again found Joshua outside the general store. "Gather your comrades," John told him. "My brother and I have decided to put on a little show of thanks for risking your lives for the colonies and liberty."

Joshua looked at him in confusion.

"Please?" John shrugged. "Umm, Gideon wants to show off."

"What kind of show?" Joshua asked.

John raised his eyebrows and tried to look mischievous. "You'll see."

Joshua laughed indulgently and did as John said, gathering his compatriots. John led the small group of militiamen to the town square where Ambrose waited.

Ambrose had five small round rocks cradled in his arm. He raised his hand in the air and walked toward the center of the dirt road. "Ladies and gentleman!" He gestured not only to the soldiers but several nearby townsfolk. "May I have your attention, please! Everyone, including my militia friends here. Please, gather round. And watch in amazement the great Gideon!"

The small band of militiamen gathered around Ambrose, several of them laughing skeptically.

John applauded. It was show time. His brother had better get this right.

Focus, Ambrose. You're a performer. Don't screw this up. If only Ambrose hadn't given his fife to their father. Then he could really give them a show. Ambrose threw one rock in the air, then two, then three, and juggled them expertly. "If only my hair were carrot red, then you'd see a fiery fool

before you. For only a fool would juggle rocks," he said loudly.

A few of the soldiers laughed.

That a boy, Ambrose.

Several more townsfolk and soldiers gathered around. John motioned for them to stay and watch.

Ambrose expertly caught the airborne rocks. "I will now foolishly attempt to juggle five rocks, and no, these rocks are not from my head." He started throwing the rocks in the air again, juggling one, two, three, then four, and finally five. "I got these rocks from the head of a British general."

More laughter.

John studied the smiling faces. Everyone was pleased by his brother's performance. Maybe Ambrose was right. Sophie was drawn to his sense of humor.

But she likes my seriousness too, right?

Ambrose grinned as the rocks soared around him like tiny, speedy moons. "I only ask one thing," he said, his eyes focused on the rocks above him. "Please don't tell King George I am so skilled, as he might send me to England as jester in his court of fools."

"This kid is a hoot," said Joshua to his fellow militiamen.

Ambrose let the rocks fall to the ground and looked pointedly at John. He might not have enough jokes or tricks to keep everyone distracted for long. John slowly backed away from the crowd and walked casually toward the corral, his heart pounding. He was almost there when a Connecticut militiaman bumped into him.

"Oh, sorry," said the soldier. His balding and sweaty scalp glistened in the sun. "What's all the laughter about back there?"

John did his best to sound casual. "Not sure, but you should go check it out."

"That's where I'm headed," said the man, striding past.

John didn't realize he had been holding his breath until a burst of air exploded through his lips. He prayed there was no one else nearby.

Holding his satchel close to his side, John walked behind the large tree and grabbed their muskets and gear. He could hear the clanging of metal as the blacksmith hammered his craft from inside his shop. As long as he kept hearing sporadic clanging and the occasional breath of the bellows he knew the man would be distracted by his work. John's heart raced as he headed for the corral's stable. He had to move fast, but not so fast that he stood out. Too much speed could get him caught.

Be smart. Don't mess this up. Ambrose would never let you forget about it. And then there's the whole hanging thing...

John gulped.

He approached the old wooden door and looked around cautiously. The black metal handle warmed his moist hand as he slowly pulled it open. Silence. *Thank God.*

John looked over his shoulder. Not a person in sight. He entered quickly and snatched the first saddle he saw in the dim light. He carried it outside, placed it on the fence rail, then darted back inside for the second saddle. A burst of distant laughter carried from the square.

Good job, Ambrose. Keep everyone there. Just a little longer.

John's heart skipped a beat as he opened the gate and carefully walked up to his chosen horse. Thankfully, the animal just eyed him, and John made quick work of tacking him up. Although Ambrose's horse shied a bit, John soon had both horses saddled and outside the corral. He placed their muskets in the holsters and mounted his steed. The horse whickered softly.

"That's a good boy. I'm your new best friend," John said. "And you are mine. At least temporarily." He gripped the lead to Ambrose's horse, gave a soft kick, and headed away from the corral, then down the road that led to General Washington.

▲ ▲ ▲

John sat on his horse off the road behind some bushes and looked back toward town. It had been at least twenty minutes. His brother should have appeared by now. What was taking him so long? He'd better not have dropped a rock on his head. What if he insulted someone?

Think positive. His brother could take care of himself. The crowd was probably throwing money at his feet.

Thankfully, a few minutes later, Ambrose appeared, jogging toward him. John smiled in relief. "What took you so long?"

"You're the slow one. I figured you'd need a lot of time."
He patted his horse, checked his musket's holster, and
mounted his steed. "I see you got the horse you wanted."

"Look closely at them both," said John.

Ambrose eyed the animals, then coughed out a laugh.
"They could be twins."

"Like us. I thought it could come in handy. Let's get out
of here." John gave his horse a nudge and led it onto the
road. Ambrose did the same and was quickly by his side.
Moments later, they were cantering along a straight path
in the woods. They traveled that way for several minutes,
horses kicking up stones and dirt. Then the path began to
wind, and thick, green pine trees surrounded them. They
slowed to a light trot.

"You should have seen me back there," Ambrose said. "If
only I had my fife."

"I thought the same thing."

"It's better off with dad. Anyhow, I walked up to this
woman, borrowed her broom and said, 'For my last trick, I
want to thank our Connecticut Militia for cleaning up the colonies from the Redcoats.' Then I started sweeping the ground."

"You're brilliant," John said. "Let me guess: the soldiers
laughed."

"Right again. Next, I balanced the broom on my forehead. I told them the key to balancing it on my head was
keeping my eyes glued to the top of the broom ... and making sure it doesn't move. And so I wanted them to keep their
eyes on liberty. If we do, we all shall have it!"

"Very clever, Ambrose."

"I flipped my head forward. The broom flew through the air. And Joshua caught it. Everyone applauded."

"Then you took a bow?" John said.

"Of course I did." Ambrose patted his horse. "Joshua said I was amazing and asked how I learned all that."

"Dad taught you," said John.

"That's what I said," answered Ambrose. "He would have taught you too, but you didn't want to learn. You were too busy with your boat building. Anyhow, they applauded, and when I thanked them, I only wished I could have said, 'And thank you for the horses.'" He slapped his thigh. "Man, that was fun. This is exciting."

John frowned and glanced nervously over his shoulder. "How long do you figure we have before they figure out the horses went missing and come looking for them?"

"I don't know." Ambrose twisted in his saddle. "Hopefully, a long time." He turned his attention to his horse. "You're very handsome. And fast." He patted the animal's neck. "But what's with this saddle? It's rougher than a cat's tongue. What'd you do — take the worst one and give it to me?"

"I took the first two I saw," John said. He swatted at a fly circling above. "I'm glad you had fun back there, but must I remind you — we just stole two horses. I hope it was the performing that made you all happy and not the stealing."

"You stole the horses," Ambrose said. "I was just the oh-so pleasant distraction."

"You're riding one. *We* stole them."

Ambrose opened his mouth, but before he could reply the brothers heard the sound of horse hoofs pounding on packed dirt. John looked over his shoulder.

A militiaman on horseback was riding toward them at breakneck speed. It was the bald soldier who had almost run over John near the corral. "Hey! You there!"

"I knew we should've stolen from a farmer," Ambrose moaned. They kicked their horses and took off as the man gave chase.

The sound of musket fire rang from behind them. With a wide-eyed glance at each other, the boys steered their horses into the forest.

CHAPTER 6

THE GOOD SAMARITAN

It had taken every ounce of Lamberton Clark's energy to stagger out of the woods. He turned right at the fork and meandered down the road. Had he done the right thing by sending the twins into certain danger? He could think of no alternative plan, but he was still fraught with worry. If only his older sons Enoch and Samuel had greater skills. And what would he tell the boys' mother?

Totally exhausted, Lamberton lost track of time. He stumbled along the road, one hand attempting to press on the wound that pained his every step. As soon as he started trekking, the bleeding had sluggishly started again. His free right hand held Ambrose's fife. He had given it to Ambrose as a birthday present two years ago. Ambrose had learned to play it quickly, which prompted Berty to give him the nickname Fifer. Would he ever be able to listen to Ambrose play again?

In the distance, a horse and buggy approached. As it drew closer to him, he fell to his knees. The fife fell from his grip and then everything went black.

Lamberton woke in a strange bed. His face, body, and pants were soaked in sweat. His shoulder was bandaged, and he lay chilled and shirtless with a blanket over him. "Where am I?" Lamberton asked groggily. The room around him came into focus. It was sparsely decorated and contained very little furniture. A man stood over him and gave Lamberton water from a cup. He drank it all and coughed.

"I got the musket ball out," the man said. "Stitched you up best I could. You've been asleep for three hours ... Used my last bottle of whiskey to sterilize your wound." He had a deep voice and tasseled mass of hair, but only on the sides. "It's I that should ask you — what happened? One doesn't often find men alone on the side of the road, shot and unconscious." The man poured another cup of water.

Lamberton reached for the jug instead, drank it all down, and took a deep breath. "A hunting accident ... My ... ahh ... son accidentally shot me. His gun accidentally went off. We were walking in the woods."

"Really?" The man raised his eyebrows. "Where's your son?"

Lamberton scrambled for words. "He ... He felt awful. He went to find help while I rested. Then I decided to try to find someone to ... help, and collapsed."

The man studied Lamberton curiously.

"He could see I'd live. I told him I'd be all right. Put yourself in his shoes … if you accidentally shot your father — "

"I'd feel awful," said the man. "But I'm not sure I'd leave you."

Lamberton sat up slowly. "I told him to. I have to find him. He's probably looking for me with help somewhere …"

"How old is your son?"

"Twenty," Lamberton lied.

The man handed Lamberton a shirt and helped him put it on. Lamberton winced as he put his arms above his head. "Thank you for helping me. I'll repay you."

The man shook his head. "Not necessary, but I'll need to replace my bottle of spirits." He frowned and put a hand on Lamberton's good shoulder. "You should stay here and rest. If that wound opens up, you'll start bleeding again."

Lamberton swung his feet around and placed them on the floor. Even with little weight, the old floorboard creaked. Lamberton felt dizzy. He tried to stand. "Where am I?"

"In my house."

"Can you or someone in your family take me home?" Lamberton would never actually have anyone take him to his real home. He'd ask to be escorted somewhere nearby. "I'll pay you for your kindness, and, yes," Lamberton grunted in a bit of agony, "I'll surely replace the spirits that I smell on my skin."

A small smile appeared on the man's face. "My wife can take you, if you insist. She's the one who found you this morning. She's not keen on the sight of blood, but she heard the tale of the Good Samaritan enough times that she had to help you."

Lamberton stood up and regained his balance. "Good thing for me she goes to church."

"Yes, and that I knew how to remove the ball from your son's musket."

Lamberton took one step forward. His knees buckled.

The man quickly wrapped his arm around him and supported him before he tumbled to the floor. "You need to rest."

"I know," replied Lamberton, in a wearied voice. "But I need to ... do it at home."

Reluctantly, the man agreed to get his wife and help Lamberton into the buggy. As the buggy bounced along the rough dirt road, Lamberton realized that he had lost his son's fife. His mind then replayed the events of the night before. He wondered who had tipped off the British that he was a spy. Or if he had made mistakes along the way that led the British soldiers to him. That he might never know the answer caused him more pain than the stitched hole behind his shoulder. Lamberton's thoughts quickly turned to his twins. *Be with them, God.* If only he were headed for George Washington instead of them. Again, he wondered if he had made the right decision. He winced as the buggy bounced over a rock, longing to know the name of the man who shot him and what he looked like.

CHAPTER 7

THE BLOODY HULL & TORY TATTLERS

Sergeant Evans and Corporal Sheffield sat majestically on a bench and enjoyed the warm breeze while two junior British Naval seamen maneuvered their small rowboat through the surf. Evans glanced back at their British sailing ship anchored half a mile off the Connecticut shore. He had shed his typical military uniform and wore instead the simple garb of a colonial farmer. Sheffield was dressed in trousers and a buckskin shirt.

The rowboat arrived on the shore directly in front of the skiff that Evans had spotted through his spyglass. Evans leapt from the rowboat, ran to the craft, and peered inside. A grin spread across his face when he spotted blood in the sloop's hull. "We have our wounded traitor!" he called to Sheffield.

Sheffield had gathered the weapons from the rowboat and was walking toward him across the sand. He tossed Evans his rucksack and handed him his firearm.

"Slice the sail, and cut a hole in the hull," Evans ordered the two junior midshipmen. "Then return to the ship, and thank the captain for his service to me. Report back that my associate and I are in pursuit of the spy."

"Aye, aye, sir," the young sailor said. His colleague had already removed his knife from his side and had begun hacking away at the white sail.

Evans knelt down on the sand and examined the footprints.

"Looks like there were two others," said Sheffield.

His sergeant's eyes filled with determination. "These rebel traitors never make anything easy," he muttered.

"Shall we kill them on sight or do you still want 'em hanged?" The look on the corporal's face revealed he preferred the first choice.

"Difficult to say ... Both have their benefits, don't they?" Evans marched ahead in the sand, keeping his eyes trained on the footprints.

Evans and Sheffield managed to find drops of blood — enough to trace Lamberton's path all the way to the side of a dirt road. There they continued to follow the sporadic brown-red drips until the trail abruptly ended. Evans stamped his foot in anger. Which way did the traitor go? Evans waved at his associate and they turned right, heading in the direction of the nearest town, which he figured was their fugitive's most likely destination.

"We need to appropriate horses at first opportunity," Evans said.

As they entered the nearby town, they casually asked questions of people they met. Had a man passed through recently, seriously injured and possibly in need of assistance? But no one in the small village knew anything about the man they sought. A few hours later, Sergeant Evans and Sheffield ventured into the local inn and inquired if anyone had seen an injured patriot. "I'm concerned for his well-being," Evans told the man at the counter.

"What's your friend's name?" asked a patron, holding a pint of stout. He had a large, bulbous nose and fat cheeks.

"I'm not at liberty to say," Evans replied, "but dare I say ... our liberty is at stake." Pretending to be a patriot was hardly enjoyable, but necessary to obtain information. Evans smiled, "He had information I need for our cause." Both he and Sheffield studied the inn's customers for any sign of hidden knowledge, but the patrons had already turned away and gone back to their conversations and drinking. It was impossible to tell if they knew more than they would say.

"Sorry. Haven't seen anyone like that," the bartender answered.

Frustrated, the disguised British soldiers exited the

room and stepped onto the inn's porch. As they were gazing out on the street and wondering where to go next, a barmaid cautiously approached them. "I saw Mrs. Halloway take someone home in the back of her buggy today," she whispered. The barmaid was plump with auburn hair that stuck out of a white cap.

Sheffield smiled at her. She grinned in return, revealing teeth even worse than his own.

"This Mrs. Halloway," said Sheffield. "Where ..."

"Down the road on the right. Her husband is the taxidermist. Sign's posted out front." The barmaid blinked up at Sheffield and smiled shyly.

Evans nudged Sheffield out of the way and stepped into the street. The corporal quickly followed, but not without a backward glance at the blushing barmaid.

"Sheffield!" barked Evans.

Sheffield leapt from the porch.

The front room of the taxidermist's house gave no sign of his occupation. No stuffed birds. No hanging deer heads. No clothing made from animal furs and hides. He greeted his two visitors and let them inside. When asked about the whereabouts of an injured person, he replied, "I'm sorry. I know nothing of the man."

Evans kept his expression casual and looked around the room. "But I heard at the inn that your wife gave transportation to someone this morning and brought him here." He peeked into the dining room. "Is your wife here?"

"She's running an errand." The taxidermist walked over to his cabinet that contained the sharp tools of his trade used for cutting hides and skin.

Evans glanced around the room for clues to the man's allegiance. Was he a patriot, loyalist ... maybe he could care less about the war? He was certainly not rich.

"It's too bad you know nothing." Evans paused, then added, "Of course, I'm willing to pay for information." Evans looked at the taxidermist pointedly.

The taxidermist seemed to consider this. He walked slowly to the window and looked outside. "Business has been slow lately and ... I am in need of some seed for new crops." He turned slowly and lowered his gaze. "You are correct ... Sometimes a trinket or more of silver gives one the motivation, let's say ..." He raised his eyes to Evans. "To share things."

Evans smiled, as did Sheffield. The sergeant opened his rucksack, took out three silver coins, and placed them on the taxidermist's table. He jingled his luggage to reveal there was more where that came from.

The taxidermist glanced at the coins. "The man my wife picked up this morning was shot by his son. A hunting accident."

"Did he have anything with him? A leather pouch or bag or any documents?" Sergeant Evans stepped forward so he was standing directly in front of the taxidermist, his eyes seeking any detection of a lie.

The taxidermist met his gaze. "No. He had only the bloody clothes on his back."

"His son shot him, eh?"

The taxidermist nodded. "Yes, and apparently ran for help. His father was quite concerned about him."

"Did you believe him?" asked Evans.

"That his son shot him?" The taxidermist shrugged. "Not sure. Accidents happen. I could see he had the worry of a father."

Evans nodded. "And where is this father now?"

"I don't know," said the taxidermist. "He left." Wanting to protect his wife, he said no more.

"His son. Did he say how old he was?"

The taxidermist nodded. "Yes. Twenty." He strolled to the table and picked up the coins.

Evans smiled. "Thank you, sir. You have been most helpful."

Outside on the road, Sheffield stopped his commanding officer. "But there were two other tracks. Either could be the courier."

"True, but we seek a young man." Evans looked back at the taxidermist's house. "The only reason for our traitor to be worried about his son is if he has the letter."

"Do we find the traitor now and kill him?" asked the corporal. "He can't be far."

Evans considered this. "No. That will come someday

soon, but right now we don't have time. We must find the courier and that letter. It's probably on its way to Washington." Evans paused and chuckled softly. "Greed is a great motivator. For the right price, even patriots talk."

"But do you have enough money?" Sheffield grunted. "It's no short distance."

The sergeant stroked his chin. "Good point. Go ... Get my money back." Evans glimpsed the pasture just beyond the barn. "And let our new greedy friend know that we'll be taking two of his horses."

Sheffield opened his mouth.

"If he doesn't give you the coins, beat them out of him."

CHAPTER 8

THE KING'S FERRY

John steered his galloping horse through the woods, dodging trees and jumping over logs, with Ambrose close behind. They hadn't heard sounds of their pursuer for the last ten minutes, but they weren't going to take any chances. If only his brother hadn't paused to tell him everything that had happened in town, John thought. They should've used that time to get further away. Fighting the urge to yell at Ambrose, John looked over his shoulder. The rider was nowhere in sight. That last detour through a ditch and some brush and past a row of bushes a while ago must have worked. John slowed his horse down and directed him behind a thicket. Ambrose and his steed followed right beside them. They halted to listen.

"I think we lost him," Ambrose whispered.

Staring through the forest all around him, John pulled on the reins and maneuvered himself closer to his brother.

"He must have given up. Headed back to town. But he's sure to tell the others and then they'll all be after us."

Ambrose nodded. For once he looked nervous. "And Joshua knows where we're heading."

John pulled out the map. He glanced up at the sun peeking through the leaves. "We're heading in the right direction. That's the good news."

"The bad news is now people know we're horse thieves."

John didn't reply. It was a label he'd never imagined would blight his good name.

Ambrose leaned over to look at the map. "We're off the road on that map and can't backtrack."

John pursed his lips. "Yeah, but if we follow the sun and keep heading south we should be all right. We've been heading the right way ..." He pointed to a spot on the map. "We should be somewhere parallel to the road Joshua marked."

The boys rode on through the trees and soon found a trail that led to a winding, dirt road. Most of the time woodlands stretched as far as they could see, but every so often a farm emerged as they made their way through Connecticut.

"This land is beautiful," said Ambrose. "No wonder so many men are willing to give their lives for the colonies."

John patted his horse and looked around at the moss-covered rocks and towering oaks. The land *was* beautiful.

"Ha! I just figured it out!" called Ambrose. "I'm naming this horse George!"

John looked over. "After the king or the general?"

"I figure it must be illegal to name your horse after the

king, so let's say the general. Although if the horse turns out to be too stubborn, then he'll be named for his royal highness for sure. But that'll be our secret." Ambrose leaned forward and rubbed between his steed's ears. "Better not be stubborn if a name means anything to you."

"There's nothing so important as one's good name." John nodded.

"That's what Dad always says."

And in an instant, the mood darkened as the boys' thoughts turned to their father. They rode silently for awhile. John gazed up at the bright blue sky.

Please, Lord, let him be all right.

"How soon do you think before they come after us for George and his look-alike you're riding?" Ambrose asked after a few minutes.

"I'm guessing we've got a good hour on them," answered John. "Assuming they've figured out what road we're on now. They can't send the whole group after us … but a scout could be on our trail, wanting these horses back."

"If they knew our business they'd leave us alone," Ambrose said angrily. He turned to look at his brother. "Don't know about you, but I'm dying to know what that letter says. What do you say we stop and open it?"

John stared at his brother. "Break the seal? Are you crazy?" He shook his head. "No way. And it's in invisible ink. We don't even know how to make that appear."

Ambrose looked at John. "You don't want to know what it says?"

"Of course I do. But if we damaged it because we were nosy, we'd have more than Dad's anger. We'd have George Washington and the whole spy ring mad at us." He couldn't believe Ambrose would even suggest such a thing.

"I bet it says how many troops the British have in New York. What kinds of weapons they have." Ambrose reached down to scratch George's neck. "That sort of thing."

"Maybe our spies are so good they even know what good old King George whispers in his sleep about the patriots."

Ambrose smiled. "There may even be a few spies out there who know about the time Sophie and I held hands."

"What?" John jerked on his reins and his mount came to an abrupt halt. "You mean about the time she and *I* held hands. And that's no secret."

Ambrose laughed. "If she touched you, it was because she thought *you* were *me*. That's the only way that ever happened."

John puffed his chest out. "She *can* tell us apart. I know that for a fact."

"I know she can too," said Ambrose, nodding.

John groaned and kicked his horse into a canter.

For two days the boys traveled through the woods, constantly wondering if someone was behind them. Using a hook and string John had in his satchel, they caught some trout in a stream, cooked them over a fire, and ate them.

Twice, they stole vegetables from a farmer's garden, though both brothers felt terrible doing it. It was never quite enough to fill them up, but it was better than nothing. At night, they slept under the stars. Since they had lost the main road, John and Ambrose wove their way along trails and other narrow roads, always in the direction of the North River. John could only hope that when they reached it, they wouldn't be too far away from the Kings Ferry. Since he carried the map, he felt responsible for their navigation, but with all those twists and turns, he was not positive how far north or south they had traveled.

When they finally reached the river on the second day, the brothers turned left and followed the river. To John's immense relief, they stumbled upon an open clearing after only a few miles. At the water's edge, a long, flat-bottomed boat bobbled on the water and bumped against a rickety dock. Logs bound by rope held the craft together. A lone ferryman carried crates of supplies from a wagon onto the ferry as the wagon driver sat perched in his seat and watched.

"Do you think the militia made it this far and clued them in about the missing horses?" John asked. He reached down and felt the satchel at his side.

Ambrose shrugged. "I guess there's only one way to find out."

The ferry operator, a man in his thirties with a bushy mustache and arms and legs the size of tree trunks, looked twice and rubbed his eyes when he saw the two boys. He waved. John was unsettled by the man's obvious interest in them. He motioned to Ambrose and steered his horse back under the cover of the woods.

"What's wrong?" Ambrose asked.

"My little voice is telling me something. I'm not taking any chances. I think it's time to put this where Dad suggested he wanted it." John dismounted. He slid his father's musket from its holster and sat down on the ground. Then he took out the leather case containing the secret letter.

Ambrose gasped as he watched his brother remove a wooden plug at the butt of the musket. A few large holes had been drilled out of the bottom of the gun's stock and covered with plugs barely noticeable to the eye. "Dad never told me those were there," Ambrose said.

"Don't be mad. I only know because I saw him make it." John carefully opened the case and took out the letter to General Washington.

Ambrose dismounted and crouched down to watch. "Looks like any normal letter to me."

"But we both know it's not," John said. With extreme care, he rolled the letter and slipped it into the hole in the stock of his gun. With a bit of wiggling, it fit — just. "There, now I feel better." He returned and tightened the plug. The grain matched exactly. This was not the first time a spy letter had been placed in the firearm. Of that, he was sure. John positioned the musket back in the holster on the horse's side and mounted his horse.

The Clark boys made their way to the ferry operator as the wagon drove away.

The ferryman looked at them curiously. "I'm seeing double."

"Yes, sir," said John.

"If only you two were identical beautiful women. Seeing one round here is rare enough." He chuckled.

"Can't help you there," said Ambrose.

The longer they stood on the road, the more nervous John felt. Somebody would be coming after them, guaranteed. They just didn't know if it would be militia or Redcoats. He looked out over the river and spotted several sailboats. *Were they patriots or Brits? Dad said they'd be searching for him. They could also be after us now.* Now that they were crossing into New York, the threat of Redcoats was much more real. There could be soldiers anywhere.

Anxiously, he locked eyes with his brother. *But did they see us?* If they'd caught their father, they could catch them too.

And if the Redcoats catch us, do we give up the letter?

"Let me guess: you boys heading for West Point?" The ferryman picked up a wooden crate from the dock and carried it to the boat.

Ambrose exchanged a quick glance with John.

"We're recruits for drummers," John said quickly. Lying never felt right.

The ferryman wiped his forehead and nodded. "One of you a fifer?"

79

"I am," said Ambrose, with a confident smile. "He doesn't play the fife. But we both drum. Looks better that way, don't you think? The enemy will see two of us and know there's something special about our battalion."

"What'll it take to get us across that river?" John got off his horse and grabbed his firearm. Ambrose did the same.

"Just that ferry and my sweat. What do you have to barter with?" The overgrown man rubbed his hands together.

John's heart sank. "Nothing really," he said. "We don't even have any money."

The ferryman laughed heartily. "You have papers from the colonial fort?" he asked.

"No," replied John.

The ferryman eyed John's musket. "That's a nice firearm. I can trade you ... one ride across for that firearm."

John pulled the musket and its contents closer to his side.

Ambrose laughed. "That gun's worth twenty rides. Why don't you just let us cross? Consider it a service to fellow patriots."

"You mean for free?" The ferryman shook his head. "I've got to earn my living somehow."

John followed Ambrose's gaze to a basket of dried beef resting on the ferry. His stomach growled. Ambrose walked up to the ferryman and looked up at him. "You a betting man, mister?"

"On occasion," he grunted as he patted George's nose. The steed nudged the man back.

Ambrose winked at John. "Where we come from we

don't judge a man by the size of his muscles or the hair on his chest, although if we did you'd surely win. No, we judge the worth of a man by his skill with a knife ... or musket." He grinned. "I bet I'm a better man than you with a knife. How about a test? If I win a little throwing contest, you give us safe passage across the river and a meal. If you win, I'll give you my friend George here." Ambrose patted the horse.

John shook his head. His brother was always the risk taker.

"We don't have much time," Ambrose said, holding out his hand. "Fair bet?"

The ferryman burst into laughter. "Fair? No. At least not for you, but it's a bet." He shook Ambrose's hand.

Ambrose took his knife from his side and carved two circular targets, one inside the other, into the bark of a nearby tree. "Here are the rules. The best out of three throws closest to the bulls-eye wins."

The ferryman removed his knife from its case on his belt. He flipped it in the air and caught it by the handle while John scraped a line in the dirt ten paces from the tree.

"You first." Ambrose indicated the line.

With a smile, the ferryman stepped up, paused, then threw his knife. He didn't even hit the tree. John watched as Ambrose held back a laugh. His confidence was clearly rising.

The ferryman ran, picked up his knife, and jogged back to his spot. His second throw hit the outer circle.

"Did you miss on purpose the first time?" asked Ambrose, narrowing his eyes.

"Maybe I did," answered the ferryman. He again retrieved his knife. "Mark my spot with your eyeballs." He returned to the line and delivered his third throw. The blade hit just inside the inner circle.

"Beat that!" he hollered. He started to go for the knife.

"No!" Ambrose held out his arm. "Leave it there."

The ferryman backed away.

Ambrose fixed his gaze on the target, rocked back, and threw his trusty knife. It soared through the air, collided with the other knife, and knocked it off the tree.

"Dumb luck!" Veins in the ferryman's neck bulged with his anger.

"Wait!" Ambrose replied. He ran and picked up his opponent's knife. Wearing a large grin, Ambrose presented it to him.

The ferryman snatched the knife from Ambrose's grasp.

Ambrose darted back to the line. "Hardly luck my friend." He stared at the inner circle and launched his knife. It flipped rapidly through the air until it connected with the center of the bull's eye.

"Yes!" Ambrose shouted. "And to think someday I'll have muscles and hair on my chest too!"

"I demand another throw," said the ferryman, his red face growing redder.

"That would be changing the rules," John declared.

The ferryman glared at John. "No throw, no chance at passageway on the ferry." The mountain-sized man crossed his arms.

"Fine," Ambrose said.

"But — " John's words were cut off by his brother's raised hand.

"You get one more throw." Ambrose pointed to the target. "You knock my knife down or manage to slide in next to it, you win. You miss … you keep your end of the bargain."

The ferryman nodded. He took his place on the mark and prepared himself to throw. His hand seemed to weigh the knife as he moved it back and forth over his right shoulder.

"Be mindful of the wind," Ambrose said. "I think it just picked up a bit. And don't forget to adjust your weight from one foot to the other. And don't forget the pressure. I am just a kid you know. Losing to me would be — "

"Shut up," exclaimed the man.

"Don't forget he does have a knife in his hand," John said to his brother.

"Good point," the ferryman replied, looking pointedly at Ambrose.

Ambrose moved closer to the ferryman so that he was standing right by his side. "I hope the point is still sharp enough to stick … if it is lucky enough to actually hit that tree. Oh, and I think the wind just changed direction a bit. Better consider that."

The ferryman shoved Ambrose away. He pulled the knife behind his ear and let it fly. It soared through the air and thudded a foot below the circle and dropped to the ground. He cursed under his breath.

"I'm glad, sir, you are an honorable man and keep your word," John said, hoping he wouldn't demand another try. If the big man refused them passage, there would be nothing they could do about it.

"Yes, we'll be sure to say kind things about you to the men at West Point." Ambrose ran and picked up his knife and cautiously handed it back to him. "He got the good looks," said Ambrose motioning to his twin. "I got a little knife throwing ability."

The ferryman cracked a smile.

Ambrose's grin met his. "Great. Now, let's get across that river!"

Moments later, John led the horses onto the ferry. "Not bad, brother," he whispered.

CHAPTER 9

HOT PURSUIT

Sergeant Evans and Corporal Sheffield had mapped out their plan to find and catch the new courier. They figured their fugitive was most likely to take Kings Ferry across the North River to New York since that was the safest and quickest passage to New Jersey.

"We will question everyone we see," Evans said as they rode. "If we move swiftly enough, we might be able to capture and kill the courier before he even reaches New Jersey. At the very least, we need to intercept him before he gets far on Ramapough Valley Road." The Rampapough Valley Road ran from Suffern, New York to New Jersey, and Evans had heard that Washington was moving his troops there. He looked at Sheffield. "It could be dangerous for us there."

"Even though we're not wearing our uniforms?" Sheffield asked.

"Less so than if we were but, still, yes." Evans kicked his steed harder and the two Brits rode their horses quickly through the dense forest. Soon they reached their first destination, the homestead of a British loyalist who had often traveled into New York City and met with Evans, providing him with information on local colonial troop movements. The simple white farmhouse featured a bright red door that signaled to Evans it was a safe place to stop. British spies often stopped to rest and feed their horses there.

"Tell those loyal to the king in New York and New Jersey to spread the word and be on the lookout for a young man traveling hurriedly," Evans said to the farmer as he accepted a plate of beans and cornbread. "He's really a patriot courier. Anyone finding him should capture him and remove any and all of his belongings. And confine him until someone on our side can smuggle him to New York City."

As he shook hands with Evans after the meal, the loyalist farmer promised to share the request through his information network. "I know of someone heading to New York this afternoon," he said. "I'll be sure he carries the news."

Evans nodded. "Also plant a seed with some patriots that a young courier is on his way to General Washington and not to be trusted," he added. "Tell them he's a loyalist spy. If we don't catch him, we can at least prevent Washington from trusting the contents of that letter."

The loyalist agreed and the men departed.

As they mounted their horses, Sheffield asked, "Do you really think he'll spread the word?"

"Gossip spreads faster than fire," Evans said confidently. "Word of this young man will spread and remain long after we capture and kill him."

Chapter 10

The Other Side

The ferry bounced in the river's current as the boys gripped the railing. John gnawed on some dried beef while he watched the ferryman hauling on the rope that extended across the river. Each tug pulled the vessel closer to the opposite shore. Beads of sweat formed like musket balls on the oversized man's brow and body.

"Victory tastes great," said Ambrose, swallowing his food. "Good thing you got those big muscles!" he shouted to the ferryman.

The ferryman ignored the comment.

John leaned close and whispered, "Once across, we ride as long as there's daylight or moonlight to see. About ten miles north is the Continental Army's fort at West Point."

"But we need to head south," said Ambrose.

"Right," John agreed. "But ... "

A large ship appeared, heading up river. Its sails were taut with wind as it cut through the water. "It's a British frigate," Ambrose noted.

"How do you know?" asked John.

"It's written all over his face," his twin said, lifting his chin at the ferryman. The burly man was pulling faster on the rope that helped the ferry cross the North River. His red face had turned white.

John studied the frigate. Her sails at full mast looked majestic in the setting sun. All aboard that ship were sworn to kill colonial patriots. Maybe they were still looking for a skiff. Or a courier spy.

Several minutes later, the ferry bumped into the dock at the opposite shore. Two Continental soldiers took hold of the towropes and secured it to the dock. Once the ferry held against the current, John grabbed their horses' reins and led them off the wooden craft. The steeds jumped from the ferry with a whinny. John loaded the muskets into the holster mounts.

"Here!" Ambrose put his hand into his pocket and took out a silver coin. He flipped it to the ferry operator, who caught it and smiled. "A tip for being so strong and getting us here safely. Thank you!"

"Where'd you get money?" John asked, his eyes wide.

Ambrose grinned. "My fans." He mounted his horse and gave a kick. "He-ya!"

John shook his head in disbelief.

CHAPTER 11

THE REDCOAT SERGEANT DRESSED LIKE A FARMER

The boys rode until the sun dipped below the tree line and the forest filled with shadows.

"I bet Mom's got supper ready by now." Ambrose pulled back on his reins, slowing his steed.

John sighed. He would do anything for some of his mother's chicken and dumplings right now. "Whoa," he said to his horse. "Hopefully, she's taking care of Dad." John bit his lip. He didn't know what to think about his dad. There was only hope.

A few minutes later, the boys dismounted and wandered off the road until they found a clearing big enough to camp in for the night. They decided not to make a fire, even though the night had grown cool. They were still too close to the ferry, and they had no idea who might be looking for them.

Exhausted, John barely said anything to Ambrose as he prepared himself to sleep. Hopefully, their journey from here on would be smooth. They still had a few pieces of jerky they'd saved from the ferry, but the brothers went to bed hungry, deciding instead to save it for the morning. John sighed deeply as he curled under his blanket and glanced at Ambrose. His twin was already peacefully asleep. John shook his head. His brother could sleep through a hurricane.

The next morning, the twins continued down the road, their stomach growling despite the jerky. After about an hour, John stopped his horse and peered into the woods. "Hey, it looks like there might be some blueberry bushes down there. I'll see if I can find us some grub."

"Fine," replied Ambrose. "I'll wait for you."

John carefully maneuvered his horse down a steep slope off the path. He dismounted, tied the horse to a tree, took out a cup from his satchel, and headed for the thick bushes. Sure enough: blueberries. One by one, he popped them into his mouth and into his cup. The sweet taste and soft crunch prompted a smile. It was just what he needed. His brother would love them too. If only they had time to hunt for birds or trap some meat. John was an expert at making snares.

The sound of cantering horses pulled John from his thoughts. Cautiously, he picked his way back up the hill to the road and crouched low. Two riders were approaching hard and fast from the direction the boys had come, but they slowed when they reached Ambrose and George. Ambrose glanced nervously at where John had left the path, his body tense.

John's heart raced. Should he stay hidden or join his brother? Who were these men? One was tall and wore the simple garb of a farmer. The other rounder man was dressed in trousers and a buckskin shirt.

"Good day," said the taller man. His greasy black hair barely moved in the light summer wind. A thick white scar marred his face under his left eye.

"Hello," said Ambrose.

"We're looking for a friend of ours," said the man in the buckskin. His voice was low and rough. "About twenty years old? Traveling alone."

"I've seen no one for miles," Ambrose replied.

John stared at the two riders. There was something in the tone of their voice and the way they carried themselves that he didn't like or trust.

"Are you sure?" the farmer demanded. He held his shoulders back and his head high, more like a soldier than a farmer. "We think our friend was headed this way from the Connecticut coast." A warning shiver tingled down John's spine.

Ambrose swallowed nervously and said nothing.

"We need to find him." The man in the buckskin shirt spat on the ground and smiled. "It's important."

John winced at the sight of his crooked, yellow teeth and held back the impulse to climb down the hill and get his gun. Instead he ducked and hoped he was low enough to remain out of sight. Fortunately, the woods were full of shade and shadows. He glanced back to where he could just see his horse grazing quietly through the trees. He didn't want to do anything to cause it to whinny or make a noise.

"Are you alone?" the farmer asked. He craned his neck to see beyond Ambrose.

'"Yes," blurted Ambrose. "I'm alone."

"You're young to be all alone, so far away from any town." The farmer maneuvered his horse closer.

"You must have rotten parents." The man in the buckskin shirt laughed.

John peeked over the ridge. Ambrose broke eye contact with the farmer and looked into the woods. "Our home's just a few miles from here."

Ambrose glanced at the man's boots. John followed his gaze and for the first time noticed how shiny they were. They were also higher than those of any farmer he knew. John put a hand over his mouth. Could these men be Redcoats?

"The young man we seek may have blood-stained clothes," the taller one continued. "If you see such a person, be sure to tell someone. We're telling everyone we see. Perhaps word will get back to us."

Ambrose looked startled. "Is he wounded?"

The farmer chuckled. "Probably not. We think our friend was with someone who was shot in a hunting accident."

"I've seen no one," said Ambrose. "Sorry."

John steadied his nerves. *Good. You've let these guys know you're done talking. Ambrose, you are smart.*

The farmer studied Ambrose. "I believe you, boy, even with your nervous twitch, and even though you didn't look me in the eye when you said you lived around here. You see, I am quite observant. But you are too young, I think, to be of good use to us."

"Or to anyone," his colleague stated. "I agree"

"I'll keep my eyes open," Ambrose said. He tried to smile innocently.

The farmer looked at Ambrose for a long time. "Be careful, boy," he said at last, steering his horse in a circle around Ambrose. "You look exhausted and these roads are dangerous for everyone, patriots and those loyal to the king. At least you have a weapon." He pulled his horse alongside Ambrose and eyed his musket. "Do you sail?" he suddenly said.

Ambrose paused. "No. Um ... I prefer dry ground."

"Me too," the farmer nodded. "Be safe, lad." He kicked his horse and trotted down the road, followed by the other man. A few hundred yards away, they turned right at a fork and disappeared into the shadows of the forest.

John exhaled loudly. *Now I see why Dad said to trust no*

one. He popped out from the tree line holding his cup of blueberries.

"Did you hear all of that?" Ambrose asked, his eyes big.

"I did." John looked down the road where the men had disappeared. "There was something ... dark about them."

"You can say that again. I'm glad you stayed hidden. I hoped you would."

John handed Ambrose the cup of blueberries and returned to the woods for his horse. He led the steed by the reins back to his brother, who had already swallowed half the cup of berries.

John mounted his steed and took out his map. "Glad we're not heading the same way they are," he said, studying the drawing. "We go straight at that fork."

"Amen to that." Ambrose put a hand over his heart. "Let's put as much distance between us and them as possible."

John kicked his horse's sides and the brothers headed down the road toward New Jersey.

CHAPTER 12

IT COULDN'T GET ANY WORSE

The twins drove their horses hard all day, galloping for miles until the light faded. Even though the suspicious men had turned down the other road, they still felt a nagging feeling of danger. Finally, the twins gave their horses some rest, slowing to a trot and then a walk.

Ambrose glanced up at the setting sun. "We'll only have light a little longer."

John grunted agreement. "We have to find a good spot for the night."

Several bats zigged and zagged over their heads, feeding on unseen insects. The horses' hoofs clicked on the rocky road. Every so often, a gap in the forest revealed a view of the river.

"The map says we have to follow the North River for several miles, then other rivers going west, then south to

New Jersey," John said, reciting from memory. "We could be in New Jersey by late afternoon tomorrow."

Ambrose, who was riding ahead of him, didn't respond. Probably too exhausted, John thought. He reached for his canteen, took several deep drinks, and secured it near his saddle. Then he caressed the stock of his musket. It reassured him to check on it periodically, to make sure their letter carrier remained right by his side.

John's thoughts drifted to that sealed piece of paper, so small yet so important. Would they be able to find George Washington? Even if they did, how would they get the letter to him? Surely he was protected — and they were just a couple of boys. And there were bears, wolves, and other dangerous predators in the area, not to mention Loyalists who would turn them over to the British if they knew what they were doing.

John looked up at the sky, which had shifted from brilliant blue to dusky purple. *I can't believe we stole horses.* The militia wouldn't let it go unpunished. Without a doubt, someone was on their trail. And if the Lobsterbacks had been searching the coast for their father, they could be after them as well.

He sighed. *Mom would say to trust God.*

The twins slowed and headed off the road into the woods, looking for a place to settle down for the night. "There's a good spot!" John pointed to a small stream. The boys stopped and tied their animals to a nearby tree. The horses lowered their heads and drank deeply from the creek and nibbled on the grass. The poor beasts were exhausted, but there wasn't much John could do about that, he realized sadly. Even the horses had to make sacrifices for the sake of the colonies. John took a few flint stones out of his satchel and started a fire. He tossed Ambrose a piece of dried beef they had been saving and they both ate the last of what they'd won from the ferryman. They took out their blankets from their saddlebags and spread them on the ground.

"I'm wiped out." Ambrose stretched himself as close to the fire as he could and pulled his blanket over himself.

"If you told me last week that we'd be doing this, I'd say you were crazy," John replied. "I'm tired too." He exhaled deeply. "I think we need to take turns staying up though, which we haven't done. After our run-in with those two men, we can't take any chances. How about you stay up for first watch?"

Ambrose threw his hands into the air. "Me? Why me? I'm just as tired as you are."

"Fine," said John. "Let's draw sticks." He grabbed two twigs from the ground and broke them into one large and one smaller piece. He showed them to Ambrose, who nodded his approval. John then handed them to Ambrose, who closed his eyes, mixed them up and placed them behind his back, where he rolled them in his fingers again. He brought his hand in front of him and placed the sticks evenly before John. John slowly pulled one out.

Ambrose opened his palm, revealing the shortest stick. He sighed. "All right. You win."

"You get first watch," said John with a grin.

Ambrose shook his head and settled his back against a tree. "Someday we have to invent a better way to decide on things. One where I always win."

"Don't be a sore loser, Ambrose." John rolled out his gear. "That's one way people can tell us apart."

"I can make it so people could easily tell us apart," Ambrose said, waving his fist.

"Ha! You like fooling people too much to ever hurt my face."

Ambrose picked up his canteen. "You're right. But I'm still way better looking than you."

"If you say so." John smiled and lay down on a blanket. He placed his musket within arm's reach, pulled another blanket over himself, and wrapped up. The sounds from the woods were soothing. Crickets. An owl. The gentle murmur of the creek. Within moments, he was snoring.

"What's that?" John said softly. He sat up, struggling to focus his eyes in the darkness. The shadowed outline of a man was tightening the girths on George. But where was the other horse? John kicked his sleeping brother, and rolled, reaching for his weapon. It was gone! He reached again and rustled the leaves. At the sound, the mysterious man turned towards John, then quickly vaulted up into the saddle.

With a surge of adrenaline that shook the last of the sleep from his body, John jumped to his feet and stumbled toward George. "Ambrose!" he shouted as he leapt and pulled the man off the horse.

George reared and snorted.

"My musket's gone!" Ambrose yelled from somewhere behind him.

John and the intruder landed a few feet from each other. Like a bobcat, the man leapt on top of him. His fist collided with John's head. Using all his might, John propelled the man off him with his legs. He grabbed a handful of dirt and flung it, but the man's hand grabbed his arm and some of it fell into his own face. Suddenly, Ambrose's body crashed into the thief and the man tumbled off John. John rolled and struggled to his knees, his head throbbing. The thief collapsed on his chest with a groan, but then he shook Ambrose off with surprising speed and scrambled to his feet, his dark eyes flashing in the moonlight.

Ambrose stood and readied his fists for battle.

"I ain't afraid of you," the thief snarled as he put up his own hands.

In the distance, John heard the blast of a musket. He turned in the direction of the noise, but could see nothing in the darkness. "There must be another one," John shouted. Taking advantage of the distraction, the thief dashed toward George, grabbed the saddle horn, and put one foot in the stirrup.

Ambrose was right behind him. John scrambled toward

their firepit and grabbed a rock just as Ambrose pulled the thief off his horse. Ambrose swung a hard right hook, slamming his fist into the man's face just below the temple.

With a grunt, John hurled his rock through the air, and it struck the man in the side of the neck — a wicked blow! It was matched by a swift kick to the groin from Ambrose that sent the thief to his knees in agony. Ambrose picked up another rock and swung it at the man's head. Blood spurted from a gash on the side of his forehead, and the man tumbled hard to the ground. He lay motionless.

John fell to his hands and knees to avoid any possible gunfire. "Get down," he ordered his brother.

Ambrose crouched beside him.

"My gun is missing," John whispered.

"Mine's gone too," Ambrose said. "Is he alone?"

John didn't move. "Nice job staying awake. I can't believe you. Of all the stupid things you've ever done — " He stopped himself and instead looked at the man on the ground. "I hope you didn't kill him."

"Shut up! All right!" answered Ambrose. "I know. It's my fault. It's always my fault!"

John looked over at Ambrose, surprised. Ambrose was staring at the would-be thief, and in the darkness John thought he saw the glitter of a tear. After a while, Ambrose said softly, "I hope he's not dead too. I don't know if I could live with myself if I killed him." Ambrose crawled into the darkness behind a fallen tree close to George who fortunately had not run away.

John followed. "It could have happened to me too."

Ambrose shook his head as if trying to clear his thoughts, then straightened up. "Your horse is gone," he declared. He studied John's forehead. "And that's some bruise."

John reached up to touch his face, but his hand froze halfway. It wasn't just his horse that was missing, he suddenly recalled. "The letter!" he cried. "The letter was in my gun!" He grabbed at his head. "It couldn't get any worse!"

Ambrose eyes grew big as he realized the enormity of the problem. "Maybe God is punishing us," acknowledged Ambrose. "Showing us what it feels like to be taken by horse thieves."

John said nothing. The two boys stood in silence for a moment, uncertain what to do next.

Ambrose leaned back against the tree, hands trembling. "Is he moving yet?"

John focused on the man. Still no movement. "No uniform. At least we know it's not the Connecticut militia." He perused the unconscious man's clothing. "Or a Redcoat. Maybe he acted alone, which means our guns must be hidden nearby. My horse could be close too."

Ambrose peered into the dark woods. "If there's another one, he's either out there waiting to take a shot at us or he left his partner behind to take George while he escaped with our muskets and your horse."

John rubbed his sleeve across the dampness collecting in his eyes. If only he had taken first watch.

Ambrose wandered around the campsite, kicking up

leaves, and searching the ground for any sign of the missing musket. "It's all my fault. We'll get —" He looked into the darkness as if searching for a word and grew serious. "You really need to name your horse. We'll get him back."

John exhaled and glared at the stars. "What does it matter about the stupid horse? We have to get that letter back." He clenched his fist in frustration and slammed the side of a tree. "Why is this happening?"

Ambrose swept an area of dried leaves with his foot. "If our weapons are hidden around here, we'll find them." He paused. "But we might have to wait until the sun comes up."

John groaned. "If you're out there ..." he shouted at the top of his lungs. "I'll find you!"

The nighttime noises fell silent. In the distance, horses whinnied. The boys looked at each other and froze. John rushed to his satchel and flung in their blankets and possessions. "Get George." He kicked dirt on the dying fire. "We'll track this guy and find him — and get the letter back."

Ambrose grabbed his brother by the shoulder. "Whoa ... wait a second. Are you forgetting we don't have any weapons? What are we going to do? Just walk up and demand he give back our horse and guns?"

John's body was pumping with adrenaline. "I don't know, but I guarantee you we are smarter than that guy. And there's two of us. And more importantly, I'm ticked." He shook off his brother's hand.

"I can see that." Ambrose took George by the bridle. "Ok. I'm with you. But maybe we'll get lucky. Maybe this thief just took your horse and tied him to a tree out there and our guns are nearby."

John shook his head. "There's more than one horse out there. You heard that. My little voice is screaming it. We'll track this other thief and find him. He has to stop some-time — and when he does ..." John bit his lip. "We just have to get that letter back." He placed his foot in the stirrup and threw his leg over George.

"What about this one?" Ambrose asked, angling his chin at the unconscious thief.

John looked at the man lying like a lump of lead. "See if he's breathing."

"What if he's faking it and grabs me? You're older, you should do it."

"Only fifteen minutes older."

Ambrose walked over to the man and cautiously nudged him with his toe. No movement. He bent down on one knee and studied the man's chest. Finally, he sighed. "He's alive."

"Thank God," said John. "Okay. Jump on. Let's get out of here before he comes to and really grabs you."

"He's gonna have some headache." Ambrose jogged to his brother, who pulled him up behind him.

John thumped his heels against George's ribs and they rode slowly into the darkness, heading in the direction they had last heard the sound of horses.

CHAPTER 13

TO CATCH
A THIEF

Mosquitoes filled the humid air as the boys trotted through the moonlit forest. They were afraid to force George to go too quickly, lest he stumble over a rock in the darkness and send them both tumbling. John quietly slapped at his neck and arms.

"I wish we had a fire stick to keep them away," Ambrose whispered.

John glanced at the moon's position. "It must be about two AM."

Ambrose grabbed John's hand on the reins. "Hold on a minute." He slid off the horse and knelt down on the trail. "Fresh manure." Inching forward, he placed his hand in an indentation on the ground. "There's more than one horse, for sure. And they're walking behind each other. Probably led by a rope."

Encouraged, the boys continued on, found a narrow trail, and followed it for another two miles until flickering red flames from a campfire broke through the darkness. Heart beating faster, John motioned for Ambrose to be quiet. They dismounted, tied George to a tree, and crept forward to check things out.

A lone man sat beside the fire. He hummed and mumbled something to himself. An owl hooted and the man twitched nervously. Three horses stood, tied to trees several yards away.

One was John's. *Maybe the musket is there too. Please, God, let it be there.*

John backed quietly out of sight, followed by Ambrose. *Keep making sounds, crickets and owls. We need you.*

Ambrose waited for John to speak. "What's the plan? I know you've got one."

John nodded. "Give me a second."

Half an hour later, Ambrose and John hid in the underbrush, watching their horse and musket thief. The man was singing "Burrowing Yankees" to himself as if trying to keep awake.

"Too bad we have to disturb him," Ambrose whispered. "Looks like he's enjoying himself."

"His singing could wake the dead." John patted his twin's back. "Time to stop it."

Ambrose took a deep breath. "If he kills me, you better kill him."

"Sure."

Ambrose started to move, but John held him back. Nodding, he closed his eyes. "Please protect us both, Lord," he whispered, then gave Ambrose a gentle shove. "Let's go." John darted deeper into the woods, keeping watch on his brother. He climbed as quietly as he could to the top of a rocky hill from which he could still see the thief below. Ambrose placed himself in the shadows about thirty feet from the fire.

John examined the small campsite. *The bandit must have all three weapons — his own, and our two — right at his side.* But only one weapon could be fired at a time. Were all three loaded? And could his brother lure the crook away from them?

Ambrose threw a rock at the thief. It missed.

The man abruptly stopped singing and looked in confusion at the stone that had landed a few feet from him.

The next throw hit him squarely in the stomach.

"Ow," he groaned as he rolled to one knee with a drawn flintlock pistol. He looked left and right and all around. "Who's out there?" He squinted his beady eyes. "Jeremiah? That you?"

"My name's not Jeremiah!" shouted Ambrose from his hiding spot in the brush.

The man stood.

John grinned. The man wasn't much bigger standing

than kneeling. He was about five feet tall and had a mass of tangled brown hair. His rough beard had dirt or food stuck in it.

Ambrose stood up, and the man's eyes grew wide when he spotted the boy. John hoped Ambrose remembered he needed to stay close to the tree.

Ambrose caressed the smooth stone hidden in his right hand. "I believe you have my brother's horse!"

The bandit cackled in amusement and mumbled obscenities under his breath. John frowned. There was something off about the way the man's face jerked with every word. He swayed slightly as he peered at Ambrose. The man was not sane.

The thief waved the pistol and shouted playfully, "Well, come and git it, then. I won't hurt ya!"

Ambrose took a half step to his left. Without hesitation, the thief raised his pistol and fired at him. Ambrose dove behind the tree as the ball smashed into the trunk, spraying bark fragments. But rather than cower, Ambrose immediately popped back out, threw his stone, and scored a direct hit to the forehead.

Stunned, the diminutive bandit shook his head. He reached for Ambrose's musket and raised it.

But Ambrose had reached into his pocket and drawn out another rock. He threw it and it thudded against the man's thigh, knocking him off-balance. Ambrose took off running into the woods, weaving his way towards the rocky hill.

The bandit yelled and chased after the boy, just as John

hoped he would. But Ambrose still needed to reach his target and create more distance between himself and his own gun in the bandit's greasy hands.

Just as John was beginning to think they might actually pull this off, the unthinkable happened — in the darkness he heard Ambrose trip, tumble, and thud to the ground with a grunt. John gasped.

As his twin struggled to his feet and started running again, the sound of gunfire split the air. From his position in the woods, John watched Ambrose jerk forward.

John's mouth fell open.

But Ambrose didn't fall. He stopped momentarily and seemed to pat the front of his shirt, as though he was sure there had to be blood gushing from somewhere. Then he looked up and continued to crash through the underbrush, the thief hot on his tail.

Seeing Ambrose was all right — or at least not dead — John remembered to breathe again. *Thank you, God! Thank you!*

Dropping the musket, the horse thief pulled out a knife and ran full tilt after Ambrose. Ambrose darted like a rabbit toward the path that headed up the hill. The thief was now only twenty paces behind him and catching up fast.

John rested on one knee as he watched the chase grow closer. If only Ambrose could zigzag to evade a thrown knife. But he needed to stay straight.

"Your little legs don't help you much, do they?" Ambrose shouted over his shoulder.

The thief's knife sliced through the air just past Ambrose's right ear and connected with a tree not far from where John crouched. Once again, Ambrose stopped dead in his tracks. He turned quickly.

John watched from a few feet away as his twin braced himself to fight the man coming toward him. The fire of hell seemed to shoot from the thief's black eyes.

Twang!

The horse thief's foot caught the snare the boys had made, which wrapped around his foot and flung him up in the air. He bobbled upside down like a caught badger.

They'd done it!

Incomprehensible curses spewed from the thief's mouth as John jumped to Ambrose's side. The twins studied their prize, speechless.

"You ... matching ... pieces of filth!" shouted the upside-down thief.

John imagined the bandit's face was redder than a Redcoat's uniform. A flurry of colorful insults continued to flow from the bandit's lips.

John raised his eyebrows. He felt immensely relieved now that the danger appeared to be over. "I don't think I've ever heard those words before." He scratched his head. "You know ... horse thieves are usually hung by their necks, not their feet!"

Laughing at his own joke, he darted back through the woods to the thief's fire and scooped up his father's musket. It was unharmed.

He aimed the musket at the rising sun and pulled the trigger. It thundered: loaded, just as he had thought. John untied his horse from the tree, took it by the reins, and slipped his musket into its holster where it nestled safely by the horse's side. John also untied the other two horses belonging to the bandits. They may have been stolen too, in which case hopefully they would head for home.

"Ha!" He slapped them on their backsides. They galloped into the morning mist. Moments later, John returned to his brother, who was holding the tiny man's knife. More ranting came from the thief.

"I take it you're not a man who reads the Scriptures," joked Ambrose.

John glanced down at Ambrose's shirt and noticed the hole on the left side. He pulled the shirt away from his twin's body to get a better look. Two holes — one going in and one going out. Ambrose looked down and stuck his finger through the holes. His mood immediately darkened.

"You could have killed me!" Ambrose shouted to the man hanging upside down before him. "Good thing you're as bad a shot as you are ugly!"

"Bad with a knife too," John added.

The thief swung at him with his fist, but Ambrose jumped back. "I wish ye was dead! You mound of festering idiot! Just let me get my hands on you!"

The thief kicked his tied leg and tried to grab at his ankle and untie it, but to no avail. "Your horses are far away, little fella." John handed Ambrose his musket, then showed the thief his own pistol. "I think this is safer with me now," he added as he secured it in his horse's saddlebag.

"Your village is missing its idiots!" The thief tried to grab Ambrose again.

"Your knife will be safer with me too." Ambrose paused. "And if you're a patriot, don't come looking for us. There's no need for revenge. We're only taking what rightfully belongs to us. Well, kind of ... Because we're ..."

"Because we're able-bodied and well-disposed young men," said John.

"Serving our country," added Ambrose.

The twins exchanged glances and nodded, then turned and hurried away.

"Your stench sickens pigs!" the bandit blurted.

"I don't think he's a patriot." Ambrose jogged over to George, untied him, and patted him on the snout.

John looked over his shoulder and shook his head. "By the way ... your idea for me to build the snare ... good one. It worked. See. You're brave and smart."

"Thank you, John," said Ambrose, with a hint of surprise.

John stared at the bandit. "We can't leave him there, can we?" He tugged on his ear. "If we leave him, he could die. We're not murderers." He gestured for Ambrose's musket. "May I?"

Ambrose handed him the firearm. John took out his ammunition and loaded the muzzle. Ambrose forced his foot into the stirrup and mounted his horse while John took aim at the thief swinging back and forth behind them.

"Right … between … the eyes," John said, aiming carefully. A look of fear appeared on the bandit's face. Arm steadied, John aimed high where the rope and tree branch met. He exhaled and pulled the trigger. The musket shot its .70 caliber ball. It soared through the air … and crashed into the rope and branch. The bandit smashed to the ground headfirst, knocked out cold.

"Now they both have headaches," said Ambrose.

John jumped onto his horse. "I was just going to say that."

He patted his horse. "Good to see you again," he said softly. He pulled his father's musket out and held it over his heart. "And especially you." He removed the plug. The letter was still in place.

Smile widening, John replaced the plug and maneuvered beside Ambrose and George. "Okay, let's backtrack to find the road that leads to New Jersey on the map."

They sent their horses hurrying westward through the woods as the sun rose behind them.

CHAPTER 14

THE GOPHER BURROW

The boys traveled a few miles away from the bandit and found a safe place nestled by a large rock to take a quick nap. After a few hours of sleep, they searched for more blueberries, but couldn't find anything to eat. John's stomach clenched from hunger. He almost wished he could eat grass like the horses. It was so much easier to find.

As the boys wandered through a field looking for edible plants, Ambrose stopped suddenly and pointed to a bush not far away. A small brown animal was just barely visible through the grass. John quickly and quietly loaded his musket. Moments later, he was skinning a hare for a late breakfast.

"We should get to New Jersey before sundown." John sat on the ground a little later rotating the spit over the fire.

Ambrose sat beside him. "I know," he snapped.

With an inquiring look, John handed Ambrose his canteen.

Ambrose took a drink. "I think I could kill a man, if I had to. Especially the man who shot dad." He picked a blade of grass. "I never thought that before."

"I'm thinking about things I never thought about before too."

"Like what?" asked Ambrose.

"Like this whole war and taxation," John said.

"Huh?" Ambrose put down his piece of grass. "I was almost killed back there and that's what you're thinking about."

"Yeah," John replied. "I've been thinking about stuff I heard dad say about it all." He paused and looked up at Ambrose. "Thank God you're fine."

"Believe me, I thanked him."

"I have too."

Ambrose picked up a stone and threw it at a tree. "Trust me. I'm thankful. Look at how close that musket ball came to me. See!" He showed John the holes in his shirt again.

John turned the hare on its spit again. "Dad would say Providence protected you."

In spite of his mood, Ambrose's expression lightened. "Dad complains about taxes, abuse of government powers, and the king taking away religious liberty," Ambrose said.

"I'm still not sure anything like this is worth dying for, brother. I find myself questioning everything."

"I don't question much," Ambrose admitted.

"I haven't noticed," John said with a hint of sarcasm.

"Don't you think the colonies should have the freedom to choose for themselves how to govern their people and worship their God?"

John glanced away. "Sure. Just not sure it's worth so many people dying. That's all."

"Dad said if you love someone you'd give your life for them. Greater love hath no one than this…"

"I know… that a man lay down his life for a friend. I know the Bible verse," John added.

"I guess those that love liberty believe it's worth dying for too," John shook his head. "People, I understand. An idea… not so sure." John smiled. "Tell you what I do know, though. Maybe someday, when I die, Sophie will be so miserable you might actually have a chance at courting her."

Ambrose laughed. "I don't need you to be dead for that. But that was a pretty good attempt at a joke. You may be more like me than you think."

"I hope not."

John took the hare off the fire and together the twins ate as much as they could manage. The meat would go bad in the summer heat, so there was no point in saving any for later. They finished just as drops of rain began to fall.

John looked up at the sky. Dark clouds were piling up in the west. The wind had picked up speed and was blowing dust from the trail. A storm was coming. Fast.

The brothers made a run for their horses.

Just to be extra sure the gun and letter stayed dry, John

cut off a piece of his blanket and wrapped it around his father's firearm.

As John and Ambrose mounted their horses, the skies opened and rain fell like judgment upon them. The July thunderstorm drenched the ground. Water dripped from John's hair onto his soaked shirt.

The boys rode for miles, in and out of rain. Several hours later, they spotted a wooden sign with Suffern, New York written in black paint but no actual town. There, the twins found a natural spring and filled their canteens.

Large pine and birch trees filled the landscape around them. The road ahead, sprinkled with puddles, had been well-traveled. The rain had stopped, for a few minutes anyway, and they plodded along through the mud. John tried to calculate how much ground they had covered in the last two days. They had to be getting close to New Jersey.

"Invisible ink. From Culper Junior." Ambrose broke the silence. "Wonder who Culper Junior is?"

John shrugged. "Probably not his real name," he said. "But he's important if Dad said to mention him."

Ambrose shook the water from his wet hair. "Think about it … If this works out, *we* get to meet the great George Washington. Do you think he's funny? I bet he's serious. But I bet I can make him laugh."

John rolled his eyes. "I doubt it."

"Is that a challenge?"

"No. Please don't do anything to embarrass me, Ambrose. This is the general. I heard he's fearless in battle... and bulletproof."

"I heard that Indians who fought against him couldn't believe their arrows or gunshots never took him down," Ambrose said.

"They say it's as if some unseen hand protects him." The boys rode in silence for a moment as they considered this. John pulled out the map and studied it. "The next road we want should be a few miles up," he said as he stuck it back in his bag. Suddenly, his horse jerked to the left and stumbled to its knees. With a grunt, John flew out of his saddle and thudded on the ground. His horse sidestepped, trying to regain his footing.

"Whoa!" Ambrose halted his horse. He jumped off George, holding onto the reins. "You all right? What happened?"

John picked himself off the ground. "Fine," he groaned. "I think he tripped in that gopher burrow there." John knelt down and gently rubbed his horse's foreleg. The horse pulled his leg away. "Easy. It's all right." John tried to soothe the horse with his voice. He caressed its leg again. No protruding bones. That was good. But the steed's ankle was already swelling slightly. Blood trickled from a small scratch.

John sighed. He led his horse a few feet by the reins and watched him carefully. "He seems okay but he's limping a bit. He needs to rest." John wanted to scream some of the curses he had heard from the bandit. Instead, he kicked the dirt, thinking through the scenarios.

They couldn't waste any more time.

He turned to Ambrose. "You'll have to go on without me."

Ambrose looked at his brother, surprised. "But Dad said to stay together."

"I know, but look, Ambrose!" John's voice cracked with emotion as he gestured toward his horse. "He can't go fast — and we have to get that letter to Washington. We don't have time to play around." John looked down the road. "It's been hard enough getting here already. Morristown is somewhere that way. You go. You have to try and find news of his whereabouts."

Before he could change his mind, John reached for his saddle and removed his musket from its holster. He walked over to George, took Ambrose's firearm out, and replaced it with his.

Ambrose looked incredulous. "What about Dad's orders?"

"The most important thing is the letter. We're too close to the finish line. One rider moves faster than two anyway."

Ambrose extended his reins to John. "Then you take George and you go. I'll stay behind."

"No. This happened to my horse. It must mean that you're to go." John caressed his horse's nose. "If it happened to your horse, then I'd have to go. So go."

Ambrose hesitated.

"Who knows what the British are doing as we speak. Dad risked his life for that letter. Time isn't a luxury we have." John tried to put on a brave face. "I'll be all right. I'll walk him for a while, and when he's ready, I'll try to catch up." John opened his satchel and took out the map. "Take this too. You'll need it."

"All right," said Ambrose, although his voice still sounded unsure. He mounted and circled George around his brother. "The road ahead leads to Morristown. Right?"

"It should," replied John.

"Okay. You catch up. Promise?" Ambrose slid his hand along the stock of their father's musket.

"Promise."

With a last solemn look, Ambrose slapped the reins onto George's back. John listened to the horse's hoofs pounding the earth as Ambrose and George disappeared. Then he took his horse by the reins and led him down the road. A lump formed in his throat.

"I did the right thing," he said to himself as he walked. "I did the right thing." His horse looked at him curiously, and something about his expression made John feel less brave than he had a moment ago. He sighed. Now it would be Ambrose who got to meet General Washington. It would be Ambrose who'd receive the proud smile from his father.

If he's still alive. God, please let him be.

Ambrose had always been the flashier one, the one others paid more attention to, even though they looked exactly alike. He could just see their older brothers congratulating Ambrose and asking him again and again to tell them about how he got to deliver their father's message — and what it was like to meet George Washington and place that letter in his hand. John knew that there were more important things to worry about, that it shouldn't matter who delivered the letter as long as it arrived, but he couldn't help but wish it were George that had gotten hurt and not his own horse.

An eagle screeched overhead. John gazed up. *Once again, Ambrose outdoes me.* He hung his head in shame. *Forgive me, God, for feeling that way.*

John glanced at his horse. "You any relation to George? Maybe you know how I feel."

The horse snorted. There was interest in the animal's eyes. John loved that about horses. He patted his steed's nose. "He's right. You need a name. You've been a great horse. And you served others, even before we took you from your owner."

A light rumbling of thunder echoed off the green hills. "Thunder. That's it. Your name is Thunder." John smiled. "Do me a favor, Thunder. Enjoy this rest. I'm going to need you to run again soon. You can do it. I've done things in the past few days I never thought possible. All over the colonies, men are doing the impossible. Even with pain. Leaving their families. Risking their lives. Getting shot and even killed." He looked Thunder in the eye. "I don't think I really appreciated it until now."

Two horses cantered up the road behind him. John

looked back at the riders as he led Thunder. The men looked familiar —

Oh no. It was too late to get off the road. He'd already been spotted. The horses slowed to a trot as they approached him.

"Good day," said the lead rider.

John turned around. It was the farmer who had questioned Ambrose two days ago.

The farmer slowed his horse further. "We meet again. You in need of assistance, young man?"

John clenched Thunder's reins. *He thinks I'm Ambrose.* "No," answered John. He indicated the horse. "He'll be all right. He just tripped in a hole. He should be okay soon."

"I thought you were going home?" said the man in the buckskin shirt.

"Um. No. I never said that," John replied, trying quickly to remember the details of Ambrose's conversation. "I just said we lived that way."

"Where do you ride from?" asked the farmer. "I don't recall asking you before."

John continued leading Thunder down the road. The farmer and his associate followed on their horses step for step.

"From near Fairfield," John answered. *Don't give too much information.*

The farmer grinned slightly. It was not a warm smile. "Beautiful area. I see you have a different horse."

He is observant. Be careful. Don't say anything. Keep walking. Look ahead.

"We've been looking for you, boy," said the other man.

John glanced up at the riders, his heart pounding. "Why?"

The farmer steered his horse closer to John. "As I rode, I started thinking about the way you reacted to my comment about the Connecticut coast, and I wondered: what if the spy we seek is younger than we were told. Out of everyone we questioned, you were the one who … well … you gave me a strange feeling. Have you slit any sails lately, traitor? Do you have anything on you that we should know about?" The farmer studied John with cold eyes.

John's pulse raced. His palms moistened as he took a tighter grip of Thunder's rein. *Stay calm. Breathe normally. Don't react.*

The farmer continued. "I thought I heard lots of splashing, but I couldn't quite tell in all the excitement. It was indeed mysteriously foggy the other morning down by the bay, wasn't it?"

Oh no. Heart pounding, John forced his face to remain expressionless. *Did one of them shoot my father?* "I don't know what you're talking about." If only he were on the other side of Thunder, near the musket.

The farmer grinned. "I'll be promoted once I obtain your message." He nodded at his associate.

The man in the buckskin shirt guffawed. "We'll make quite an example of you, boy. We have no issue hanging rebel spies, even young ones. Isn't that right, Sergeant?"

"Indeed we don't, Corporal."

John fought the fear creeping into his bones. His mind raced. If he told them about the letter, maybe they'd let him go. They could catch up to Ambrose. But no, he couldn't do that to his brother, to his country. So what were the other options? What if he fought back? No, again. He didn't stand a chance against these two armed men, and with an injured horse, he couldn't run away. Besides, a piece of paper wasn't worth dying for. Or was it? If only he knew what the letter said!

"How was your trip across the Sound? Quite fun? We found your blood-stained skiff. Was it a relative of yours that was shot? Perhaps an uncle? Older brother? Or father?"

John scratched at his ear. "I told you I don't know anything about that." He looked ahead.

The two men exchanged glances. As fast as a striking snake, the farmer slipped off his horse and snatched John by the arm. Thunder leapt into the air, jerking the reins from John's hand. The other man rode up alongside Thunder, secured the beast, and grabbed the reins of his partner's steed as well.

"Allow me to introduce myself," sneered the man. "Sergeant Conrad Evans of His Majesty's Royal Army. And I don't believe you."

John forced his arm up hard to break from the sergeant's clutches, but Evans' grasp was too strong. Evans dragged John to the side of the road, several feet into the woods.

"Let go of me!" demanded John. "I've got nothing to steal. No money! Nothing! Just my horse." Close to panic, he kicked at Evans.

"You're a rebel and a spy." Evans clutched John by the shirt and smashed his fist into John's face. "And you have what I want." He pulled John closer to him.

John's face and head ached from the blow. He fought to stay conscious, sagging in the man's arms, and blinked at the eyes in front of him. Pale blue eyes. Cold and without compassion.

His partner tied the three horses to several saplings. The sergeant gestured for him to check Thunder's saddlebag and satchel, and he quickly obeyed. He spat periodically as he rummaged through it all, dumping John's possessions onto the ground. After a few minutes, he looked at Evans and shook his head.

"Where's the letter, rebel traitor?" With John firmly in his grasp, Evans did his best to frisk the boy with his right hand. When he found nothing, he threw John to the ground. John groaned as his aching head struck the dirt.

"Corporal Sheffield!" the commanding officer bellowed and his subordinate rushed to his side and presented him with Ambrose's musket. Evans examined the weapon then tossed it down. "Check his shoes," barked Evans.

Sheffield bent down and grabbed John by the foot. Although he was dazed and knew it was probably in his best interests to cooperate with the men's search, John was too outraged to go down without a fight. These could be the men that chased after them in New York. One could be the Redcoat who shot their father. Anger boiled inside him. "Leave me alone!" Mustering his strength, he swept the heel of his foot across Sheffield's face. The soldier barely flinched, grinned, and spat out a bloody tooth. He then snagged John's foot and ripped off one cowhide shoe and then the other.

Meanwhile, Evans took out a musket ball and powder and began loading his musket.

Sheffield carefully examined the inside and bottom of John's shoe. He playfully winced at the smell and threw the shoes at John's head. "This rebel is more like rabble," he said with a scowl.

Evans leaned over John and began kicking him methodically in the side. Hard.

"Unhh!" John folded in on himself, trying to protect his ribs. For a few never-ending seconds, the pain that blossomed in his side was nearly unbearable. But then the kicking stopped. Shifting, John cracked open an eye.

The sergeant now aimed his gun at John's head. "Where's the letter you little — filthy — rebel? Don't think I won't kill you. I've thought of nothing but finding and killing you my entire ride."

John gazed up the barrel of the musket. *Tell them Ambrose has it. No. What would Dad do?* "I don't know what you're talking about," John whispered at last. "I'm just a kid."

Sheffield snorted in disgust.

Dad risked his life for that letter. John gazed at the disguised Redcoats. *So will I.* Once again he kicked at his captors, nailing Sheffield in the shin.

Evans kicked John hard again as Sheffield staggered backward, wincing. "A kid who loves his father, no doubt," Evans sneered. "But what kind of man would send a boy to do a man's job?"

"Those aren't the boots of a farmer," John said, struggling to sit up. He spat on them. "You're not that smart. You'll never find what you're looking for." Immediately after he spoke, he feared he had said too much. He hadn't meant to admit to knowing any information.

Again, Evans raised his weapon at John. "I'll find that letter, boy. Even if I have to tear everything you own apart after I kill you. It's here somewhere. You didn't finish your job yet. And after I kill you … I'll go back to Connecticut and kill your father."

Trembling, John braced himself for more pain.

"Do you have a mother, boy? I'm sure she is lovely …" The British soldier's breath was heavy and every odorous syllable sent a chill up John's spine.

"I have three older brothers," John said, barely able to contain the rage in his voice. "One of them will stop you and kill you, if they have to." He reached to grab his captor's leg, but the Sergeant kicked away his hand and delivered another sound blow to his ribs with his foot. John gasped for breath, wondering if his ribs were cracking. Blurry-eyed, he focused on the scar on Evans' face.

"You like my scar? Remnants from a bayonet fight with an American colonist who didn't live to tell the tale of the encounter." Evans spat on John's face. "You defiant little pig." He kicked John's side again, and this time John couldn't even muster the strength to protect himself. "You and your father are thorns in my flesh. I think I'll enjoy killing you more than any other patriot scum." He nudged the muzzle of his weapon against John's chest. His blue eyes closed to slits. "Before I kill your father I'll show him that I did indeed kill you. What part of you shall I bring to him? Perhaps your finger? Or your ear?"

"His scalp," said Sheffield.

Evans pulled his weapon back and pushed a button. A blade popped out from beneath the barrel. He sliced John's face just inches from his eye. Searing pain followed by warm blood dripped down John's cheek.

"For the last time ... Where's the letter?"

Hairs rose on John's neck. *Lord help me*, he prayed and prepared himself to meet his Maker.

CHAPTER 15

WORTH DYING FOR

Evans cocked the musket and positioned it to fire. As his finger closed on the trigger, he suddenly screamed in agony and dropped the weapon. Evans raised his hand — a knife's blade was sticking through it and blood ran down his arm. John looked in the direction from which the knife had come. Ambrose stood on the road about fifteen yards away, wearing a satisfied grin. Evans looked like he had seen a ghost.

"Brother!" Despite the pain in his ribs, John felt a new surge of hope and energy. He swiped Evans' legs out from under him with a sidekick and ripped the gun from his hand. Before Sheffield could react, John had aimed Evans' musket at Sheffield and pulled the trigger. The musket ball ripped Sheffield's flesh at the knee, spewing blood and buckling the man's leg.

Evans pulled the knife from his stabbed hand with a scream and lunged at John, blade flashing.

Fire from another musket rang out. Evans jerked back, groaned, and fell backward to the ground, clutching his shoulder. Smoke from the fired weapons filled the air.

Hissing in pain, John picked up the knife from where Evans had dropped it and held it in shaking hands while Ambrose reloaded their father's musket. He locked eyes with his twin. "You came back? What are you? Crazy?"

Evans struggled to raise himself to his knees, while Sheffield stood clutching his bloody leg, frozen in place. Both moaned in agony.

"Good thing I did," Ambrose said. "You didn't have this situation under control." He studied John. "Your eye is swelling. All black and blue too."

John moved closer to his brother, keeping an eye on the incapacitated Redcoats. "But why? Why'd you come back?"

"I kept thinking about what Dad said: stay together. Something just didn't feel right about me leaving. It was *my* little voice."

Before they could say anything more, the sound of a galloping horse came up the road.

Sheffield had torn his shirtsleeve off and with shaking hands was wrapping it around his knee to stop the bleeding. Evans had his bleeding hand in one armpit and his other hand over his bleeding shoulder, trying to keep pressure on both wounds. Neither man was going anywhere fast. Evans

stood up shakily and shouted, "You rebel scum don't know who you're dealing with!"

The rider came into view and came to a stop. "You? I found you!"

It was Joshua. He had indeed followed the trail he'd given them with the map. "Whoa!" Joshua reined in his horse and jumped down, immediately grabbing the musket from his horse's holster and pointing it at them. His face reflected a mix of relief and anger. "I should shoot you right here for stealing our horses . . ." he began. Then he saw John's battered face and noticed the two bleeding men. He sucked in a breath.

"Yes, please do," moaned Sheffield. "Shoot these traitors. Give me your gun. I'll kill them for you."

Joshua peered at the injured man leaning against the tree. A look of disgust crossed Joshua's face, followed by confusion.

"They're stealing our horses," said Evans through gritted teeth. "Shoot them. Shoot them both. Now!"

The young private aimed his musket steadily at Ambrose, who quickly lifted his musket and aimed it back at Joshua.

"We're not horse thieves," said John. The burst of adrenaline that had enabled him to escape from Evans had faded, and each breath felt like a fresh kick to the ribs. He lowered himself to his knees.

"Yes, they are," Evans grunted. "Shoot and kill at least one of them now before they shoot you!"

"They're Redcoats," John blurted. "They tried to kill me.

We borrowed your horses because we're on your side and on a special mission."

Joshua's hand wavered. His eyes searched the boys for truth.

"They're lying," Sheffield cried. "He shot me in the knee."

"What special mission?" Joshua asked. He lowered his gun just slightly.

"We can't tell you," Ambrose replied. His arms were shaking and John knew he must be getting tired from holding the musket on its target for so long.

Joshua shook his head. "I'm sorry, boys. You're going to have to give me more than that."

Evans sneered. "We were just traveling down the road when they ambushed us. Don't believe them."

John looked at Ambrose, gnawing on his lip. *Should they tell Joshua the truth?* As if in confirmation, Ambrose nodded.

John turned back to Joshua, speaking quickly. "Joshua. We're going to trust you. Our father is a courier for the Continental Army. He gave us a letter to deliver to General Washington. That is our mission. We still have to complete it." He pointed at Evans and took a painful breath. "That man shot our father, which is why we shot them — to protect ourselves. You have to believe us. We're telling the truth."

Joshua looked at John, then the two wounded men, then Ambrose, then back at the disguised Redcoats. Finally, a small grin appeared on his face. Ambrose lowered his musket. Seeing that, Joshua relaxed his aim, then stiffened when Ambrose raised the musket again. This time, however, Ambrose pointed his weapon toward Evans and paced over to him.

"You. You're the man who shot my father?" His eyes flared with anger.

John stood and took a step closer to Ambrose. He'd never heard his brother sound so angry.

Ambrose placed the end of his musket against Evans' Adam's apple. Evans gave Ambrose a look that practically dared him to squeeze the trigger.

"Don't kill him," John said quickly.

Ambrose's finger began tightening on the trigger. "I'd be doing the cause of liberty a favor."

"Brother ..." John touched Ambrose's elbow, but Ambrose shook him off.

Joshua tightened his grip on his own weapon.

"Ambrose." John tried again. "Don't do this. This isn't who you are. This isn't who *we* are."

A long moment ticked by. Then, with a growl, Ambrose released his finger. He turned toward John, then spun back around and swung the stock of the gun at the sergeant's face, sending him to the ground. Blood gushed from the Brit's nose. Ambrose turned to Joshua with a bow. "I present you two Redcoat Lobsterback prisoners of war. You may kill them if you like."

Joshua aimed his weapon at Evans and Sheffield. "I

believe you. If nothing else, I can tell by his boots." The private nodded at Evans.

Exhaling, John lumbered to find his shoes. Hissing through the pain of bruised ribs, he leaned over and slipped them back on before limping over to Thunder. He looked at Joshua. "We have a mission to complete. Think you can handle them?" He nodded toward Evans and Sheffield.

"No problem," the private replied. The wind had picked up and drizzles of rain began to fall again.

John walked his horse over to his brother. He winced in pain. "This is Thunder."

"You named him?" said Ambrose.

John smiled.

"Where's Buttercup?" called Joshua. "He's my horse."

"You named your horse Buttercup?" Ambrose shook his head in disbelief. "The horse of a militiaman is *Buttercup*?"

"That's his name," said Joshua. "And I want him back."

"I tied him to a tree back over there," Ambrose gestured. "He's a good horse, makes great time. After we find General Washington, we'll return him to you. I promise."

"What's this one's name?" John asked.

"Thunder," said Joshua. "You said it before. Why are you asking? Perfect name for him."

John looked at Joshua in amazement. Then he smiled. "Yes, it is," he said. "Yes, it is."

Ambrose turned his attention to their prisoners, who were scowling and clutching at their wounds. "You have some rope?" he asked Joshua.

"Saddlebag." Joshua gestured with his head.

Ambrose walked to the private's bag and took out the rope. Wiping the blood from his knife blade onto his trousers, he cut a few pieces. He went first to Sheffield, ripped Sheffield's sleeve from his shirt, and tied his hands behind his back. He then jogged to Evans, who was still standing with his bloody hand in his armpit and his other hand over his shoulder. Ambrose flung Evans' hand off his shoulder and wrapped and tied a piece of Sheffield's shirtsleeve around it to help stop the bleeding. He secured both of the sergeant's hands behind his back. The man seemed to have lost his fight and stood in stony silence.

"That's the knot of a sailor," Ambrose said fiercely. "My father taught me. You'll need twenty fingers or an axe to get it undone."

Ambrose moved to stand in front of Evans, toe-to-toe, recoiling slightly from his foul breath. "Your prisoners are secured," Ambrose said to Joshua. "I wish we could stay and help you, but we have a message to deliver."

"Understood," Joshua said. "It'll be my honor to bring the Redcoat scum to the Continental Army."

John went to Thunder and pulled himself into the saddle, wincing in pain. He imagined he'd feel even worse in the morning. Nothing to be done about that, though. He reached down and helped Ambrose up. "You have the letter?"

Beaming, Ambrose raised the musket. "I left George that way." He pointed down the road. "Well out of sight and sound, so I could rescue you. The road back there was rough. Good thing too. It made me travel slowly, so I heard the yelling. Realized I needed to keep George away so I could sneak up."

John nodded a thank you and looked back at the private, who was prodding Evans and Sheffield to move as he secured their horses.

"You're brave, brother," Ambrose said. "And I am getting smarter. Better watch out. Maybe someday I'll be as smart as you."

"Maybe we're already more alike than we think," John replied.

Ambrose studied his brother's bloody cheek. "If that scars, we won't be identical anymore."

Wiping the blood from his face, John nodded sadly. "Yeah. I thought the same thing." He tapped his heels into Thunder. "We better find the general soon."

Ambrose held on to his brother as Thunder started at a walk toward George. "He's not limping anymore, but his leg's still a little swollen," John said, patting Thunder's side. "I don't want to push him too hard yet." John turned to look at Ambrose. "Maybe when we reach George, you should gallop on ahead again. Carry the letter to Washington."

Ambrose shook his head. "No way, brother. I'm not leaving you behind." He grinned. "You need me. We'll reach Washington together, one way or another."

When they reached George, Ambrose jumped off Thunder and climbed into the saddle. "To the general, big brother. Lead on!" he shouted.

CHAPTER 16

THE ROAD
TO THE GENERAL

On horseback, covered in mud, soaking wet and shivering, John and Ambrose made their way down Ramapough Valley Road. Thunder appeared to be doing fine, though they hadn't attempted to gallop yet. The boys trotted through small timber for ten miles before finally coming out before a long valley. Both of them gasped. Ambrose let out a low whistle.

Below them to their right, row after row of tents and ragged soldiers clustered around small campfires. The boys descended into the valley, riding past tents and soldiers who dipped their canteens in the river at the base of the green mountain range.

"The Continental Army," said John in amazement. "You know what that means?"

Ambrose stood up in his stirrups and looked down the road. "Washington must be close. I can feel it."

"Me too." John smiled.

John looked at the soldiers busy about their tents, cleaning their guns or cooking food. A few looked up and nodded as the boys passed. Many were barefoot. Others wore shoes that were held together by rags. John glanced down at his own boots, feeling suddenly ashamed at the apparent extravagance. *Mother wanted to throw these out months ago. And yet they're so much better than what these men have.* John thought about Evans' sturdy boots. British soldiers were certainly better equipped than the Continental Army.

Ambrose broke the silence. "The tents are never ending."

"There must be thousands of them."

The tents had seen better days. Many had holes and looked weather beaten. "And there must be hundreds of wagons," Ambrose added.

A soldier near the road walked briskly up to them, and the twins stopped their horses. John figured the soldier was in his early twenties. He had blonde hair and a tattered blue uniform. A bandage was wrapped around his right bicep. He jerked a nod as if to say, "What are you doing here?"

"We're couriers with a special message for General Washington," Ambrose declared.

"Is he in camp?" John scanned the field for a special tent that might be suited for a general. But they all looked equally old and tattered.

The soldier studied them suspiciously for a moment, but then shook his head. "No, the general's down the road." He pointed. "Always protected by his life guards unit."

"Thanks," the twins said in unison. They gave their horses a kick and trotted further down the road. Soon, the troops' tents dropped out of sight, and they were once again flanked by woods on both sides of the road.

A little further down the way, two armed sentries stepped from the trees and approached the twins from their right. They wore tan pants, white shirts, and navy blue jackets with yellow trim. They looked important. Both had pistols aimed at the brothers.

"Whoa," the Clarks said in unison. Their horses halted.

The soldiers looked from Ambrose's face to John's. Before one of them could speak, Ambrose interrupted. "Yeah, yeah, we know — we look alike."

"Indeed," said the shorter soldier with black hair. "Other than the black eye and blood. In any case, I'm afraid you won't be going any farther."

"This is a secure area," added the other soldier. He had red hair and long, thin legs. "We just set up camp down the road, as you saw, after a long trip from Morristown. From here on, the road is closed. Come back in a day or two and you'll be able to pass. But this afternoon you'll have to find another route to wherever you're heading."

"We have an urgent message for General Washington," John said. He could only pray these soldiers would take them seriously. "You have to let us through or bring us to him. Immediately."

The two sentries glanced at one another. The shorter one

looked confused. "I thought there was only supposed to be one," he whispered to the other sentry.

The tall one shrugged and pointed at George. "But the horse," he said. "It has to be." John suddenly had a bad feeling. "What's going on?" he asked, looking from one to the other. "What do you mean?"

The short sentry straightened up and raised his musket. "Throw down your weapons and dismount from your steeds," he said. "Now."

The taller one also raised his musket. "You're under arrest." Both the sentries looked deadly serious.

"What?" said Ambrose, his voice high with emotion. "You're joking, right? What did we do?"

"Wrong question," the taller one added. "What were you going to do?" He waved his musket for the boys to dismount their horses.

The twins slowly got down from their steeds and raised their hands.

The black-haired sentry glared at the two of them. "We got a tip from someone that a young courier might soon be riding into camp with a message for Washington but that he was not to be trusted."

"What?" exclaimed Ambrose.

John bit his lip. It had to have been that British Sergeant who spread the rumor. Even now, when they were so close, he was a thorn in their side. Maybe Ambrose should have shot him.

"Sir, we've been through hell to get here," Ambrose insisted, taking a step toward the soldier.

One look told him to halt.

John nodded. "Our father's been shot. He's the real messenger." He looked each soldier in the eye and fought to maintain his composure. "We're the only ones he could trust. You have to believe us." A tear welled in John's eye. As quickly as it appeared, he wiped it away.

George began to walk away and Ambrose quickly grabbed George's bridle. "We've stolen horses, fought bandits—"

John's plead overlapped his brother. "We captured two Redcoats who were after us down the road."

"They're under the guard of a Connecticut militiaman now," Ambrose interjected.

"We're telling the truth." John's voice cracked. "You have to trust us. Please. We have to see the general."

The sentries looked at one another. "Give me the message," the red-headed sentry said at last. "I'll get it to the general."

Ambrose hesitated. "No. We know you're on our side, but we were instructed to trust no one." He looked up at John.

John nodded. "This message must go from our hands to the general's."

John stood next to Ambrose. "You have to trust us. Look at my face." He touched his cheek. "I've been beaten. All for this message. Now, we have to get it to the general. Please." A light rain began to fall once more, and the cool drops brought momentary relief to John's throbbing eye and cheek.

"Nice story, but we have orders," said the red-headed sentry. He waved his weapon at the boys. "We have a holding area waiting for you. Major Gibbs will deal with you next."

"Who is Major Gibbs?" John asked.

"He's second in command after Washington," the taller soldier stated as he pushed the barrel of his musket against John's shoulder ordering him to move forward.

The red-headed sentry took the bridles of the boys' horses and led them down the road, while his partner fixed his musket on the twins' backs. They escorted the twins one mile down the road. Soon, the boys spotted a Dutch-style farmhouse nestled between a pond and a mill. Covered wagons stood outside and several men were unloading what appeared to be artillery and supplies. Four members of the Continental Army stood guard.

"General Washington must be there," John whispered to Ambrose.

"Quiet!" the taller sentry exclaimed. "The holding area is behind the barn."

As John, Ambrose, and the sentries approached the house, the black-haired sentry addressed another guard. "Where is Major Gibbs?"

"He's not here," a guard declared, eyeing the twins curiously.

"We must see the General!" John shouted. He hoped his comment would initiate a response revealing that the general was indeed inside.

Voice full of emotion, Ambrose shouted, "We have to see him!"

"Shut your traps!" the red-headed sentry ordered. He raised his weapon at John.

"General Washington is not to be bothered," said one soldier with thin lips and a pale face.

"Then let us see Gibbs!" Ambrose called out.

John put his hands in the air. "You have to trust us."

Ambrose lifted his hands too. "We were sent here by our father, who is a courier out of New York."

The guards quickly overmatched and grabbed them by their arms. The black-haired sentry and another guard clutched John's arms behind his back and led him away from the house. "To the holding area. You will see Gibbs later, young man."

"Take us to him so we can explain the situation and deliver our father's message to General Washington," John exclaimed, full of frustration. As he did so, the skies seemed to open up and rain fell like a curtain all around them.

From the south, several men now arrived on horseback, led by a short and stocky Dutchman with wisps of silver hair. He dressed like a private citizen. John marveled at the navy blue jackets with yellow trim the other men wore. Tall black hats with short brims suggested they were high-ranking soldiers.

A major with combed back dark brown hair and a noble nose followed. In the center of the group, protected by the others and riding on a tall white horse, was a man in the same full dress uniform of the Continental Army. As soon as they laid eyes on him, the Clark boys knew — this was General George Washington.

"What is going on here?" the Dutchman asked, taking in the struggling twins and their captors.

John pulled against the arms that were restraining him. "General Washington!" he yelled. "We have a message for you!" A hand clamped forcefully over his mouth and he was unable to say more. With a last surge of energy, John spun and escaped from the soldiers' grasp, only to be tackled a moment later. He landed heavily on his stomach and lost his breath. A soldier sat on his back. John gritted his teeth as his bruised ribs began to throb once more. But at least now his mouth was free. "I have a message from Culper Junior for you!" John shouted again.

The black-haired sentry stood before the group of officers and saluted. "We have captured the spy that you received a tip about this morning, Major Gibbs," he said.

Soldiers surrounded Washington as he dismounted from his horse.

"Get the general into Mr. Van Allen's house," said a soldier with a bony body and sharp nose. Washington ignored the commotion as four of his guards hurried him into the home.

"Take these two away! And gag the noisy one," said the soldier near Ambrose. He cocked his pistol and aimed it at John. "The general has his Life Guards always around him. You're crazy to think you could get to him."

"But I'm not trying to kill him!" John said, his voice cracking with emotion. "I already told you!"

The trooper holding Ambrose took out some rope and began tying his wrists.

John tried to get up, but the soldier sitting on top of him pushed his shoulders down. "Ow!" John grunted as he hit the ground again with a thud. Two men forced him on his side and began tying his wrists. "Stop! You don't understand!" John cried. The men ignored him.

Frantic, John glanced around in time to see the well-dressed major look over at the twins as the sentry talked to him. Major Gibbs studied the soldier pinning John with his foot. "Take them to the barn," he said loudly. "And keep them tied up until I can talk to them."

One soldier grabbed each of John's arms and pulled him to his feet. Next to him, Ambrose struggled against his own captors. "But we're on your side," he pleaded. "We're on your side!"

The sentries dragged the twins to the holding area behind the barn, which sat fifty yards from the house. The rough rope scratched at John's wrists as he tried hard to wiggle his way out. But it was no use. The soldiers knew too well how to secure a prisoner. The strong scent of manure from the barn penetrated John's nostrils. Feeling cramped and exhausted, all he could do was give Ambrose a look that said, "What else could go wrong now?"

CHAPTER 17

NOTHING MORE SACRED THAN GOOD INTELLIGENCE

Ten minutes later, the wooden door opened and the black-haired sentry appeared with his colleague whose musket was aimed and at the ready.

"Major Gibbs will see you now," the taller one declared.

John sighed. He turned to Ambrose with hopeful eyes. He had expelled all his energy explaining their story numerous times. Could he or his twin convince the major?

The soldiers escorted the twins outside the barn, down the road, and to the house. John paused as he looked at the front stairs. *Please, God, help us.* A musket's barrel nudged his back and he walked up each wooden plank and inside.

They entered the parlor where several of Washington's Life Guards stood. John looked for the general but did not see him. Instead, Major Gibbs stood near the fireplace with his hands behind his back. He looked at the boys not with the hostility they had expected but with curiosity.

"Release them and untie their hands," Gibbs told the solders. "And give them each a hunk of bread. They look famished."

John glanced at Ambrose. He thought they had been brought here to be interrogated or punished. Maybe Major Gibbs believed them after all.

John looked around at the room while one of the militiamen ran off to find the bread. Blue and white plates with windmills painted on them filled the hutch that stood against one wall. They reminded John of his mother's special little dish that sat in the family's parlor. A Bible lay open on a table. John craned his neck to get a better look. The words were written in some language he didn't understand. A cushioned chair flanked the fireplace. On the opposite wall, there was a doorway leading to another room, but John was unable to see inside.

Major Gibbs did not speak again until the militiaman returned with the bread. He dismissed the soldiers and turned back to John and Ambrose as the boys did their best not to eat too quickly. John's stomach fluttered. They had come so far. Been through so much. Would the Major believe them? He brushed the dirt from his sleeve and stood erect.

"So …" The major paused.

"We must see General Washington," the twins said simultaneously.

"We have a message for him," John added.

"Yes," the major said. "We heard. From Culper. That name is the only reason you're standing here right now."

John and Ambrose exchanged a brief look. So that was why the major seemed to trust them when no one else would. He must know about the secret code name.

"The message is hidden in the stock of my musket," said John. "The sentries took it from me. I don't know where they put it, but I must get it back."

Major Gibbs signaled to one of the Life Guards who quickly ducked outside into the drizzle. "We'll get your gun back," the major assured the boys.

Relieved that finally someone believed them, John leaned to his right and tried to see in the opposite doorway. Where was General Washington?

A few minutes later, the Life Guard returned with both John's and Ambrose's muskets. He set them on a table near Major Gibbs and saluted.

"It's the one on your left," said Ambrose helpfully through a mouthful of bread.

The major picked up the musket and examined it curiously but said nothing. The sound of the crackling fire and the tap of rain on the windowpanes were the only sounds in the room.

Just as John was wondering what was going to happen

next, a strong voice called from the next room. "You may bring them in."

John and Ambrose exchanged looks. John's heart beat faster. Could it be General Washington?

The major motioned the twins towards the doorway at the other end of the room.

The boys slowly walked forward. As they peered around the door, they saw Hendrik Van Allen, the Dutchman, sitting in a chair in the corner of the room. But they barely even noticed him. Their eyes were locked on the tall, elegant man writing at a portable desk. General Washington. A few letters and documents were laid out neatly on the table next to him, and Washington brought one letter closer to the light from two brass candlesticks. John had to remind himself to breathe.

When the twins entered, Washington and Van Allen stood up.

John compared the height of the general with the height of the ceiling. *Father was right.* Washington was indeed tall, well over six feet. He had a commanding presence. His white wig gave him an air of wisdom and nobility. He held his lips tight together and his face was serious and a little bit sad, as though he carried a heavy burden. John knew he stood before a special man.

"You boys have been through quite a squabble," Washington said. His eyes fell on John's cuts and bruises. "Especially you."

"You should see the other two guys," Ambrose said.

Did Washington just crack a quick smile? As fast as it may have appeared it was gone.

"Welcome to my headquarters," said Washington. "At least for a day or two. We just arrived today. The Ponds. That's what they call this area."

"Thank you, sir," the boys said in unison.

"This is my friend Hendrik Van Allen," Washington said. "This is his home and he has kindly offered it as our camp."

The twins nodded, acknowledging the Dutchman.

"And you've already met Major Gibbs." Washington gestured to his senior officer who stood behind John. "Gibbs is in charge of my Life Guards. He is responsible for protecting me wherever I am."

Ambrose turned to nod at the major, then faced Washington. "We have a message from Culper Junior," he said urgently.

"In invisible ink," John added. 'It's hidden in that musket," John pointed to his father's gun which Major Gibbs still held.

Washington said nothing but beckoned for Major Gibbs to hand him the firearm.

John still couldn't believe he was with the commander in chief of the Continental Army. "You have to turn that wooden plug loose to remove the letter, General," John said, pointing toward the butt of the musket.

"You wouldn't believe what we went through to get this to you," Ambrose said.

155

Washington raised his eyebrows and kept his focus politely on the twins. "So how did two boys get enlisted by Culper Junior to do our handiwork? I must correspond with him about such tactics." He paused. "You boys are a trifle young."

"Our father was shot," John said. At the thought of his father, a lump formed in John's throat.

Ambrose nodded. "He had no choice but to send us."

"Is he well?" The general looked concerned.

John shook his head. "We don't know."

"We had to leave him to get this to you," Ambrose added. "He said this was much more important than he was." He nodded at the musket.

The general worked on the plug with his index finger and thumb. Soon, he pulled it out of the musket.

John sighed in relief. He could tell the wood inside — and everything else — was bone dry.

The general reached inside a compartment in his writing table and pulled out a device that resembled tweezers. "There is nothing more necessary than good intelligence to frustrate a designing enemy and nothing that requires greater pains to obtain." Washington used the tweezers to remove the letter from the secret compartment.

"Pains?" Ambrose showed off the bullet holes in his dirty shirt. "I was shot at."

Washington nodded. "Looks like the all-powerful dispensations of Providence protected you."

Washington broke the seal and unrolled the letter. It was

written with black ink in a flowery hand and looked like nothing so much as a love letter.

"We need express riders like your father," Washington continued, "and like both of you, to help us win this war, which is as much a battle of wits and wisdom as it is a battle of might."

He carefully held the letter before the flame of a nearby candle. Seconds later, almost magically, secret nut-brown words appeared in between the lines of the original letter. Washington read them silently.

The boys stared. Would he tell them what they had risked their lives for?

The general drew a deep breath and gazed out the window for a moment. "It seems there's a plan to kidnap and kill me." He paused and looked at the boys. "This letter contains the names of several loyalists for us to watch out for."

"I'd say that was an important message then," said Ambrose.

John agreed. Worth risking a life for. *The colonies need General Washington if we're to win. Dad said so.*

"Yes, indeed," said General Washington. "Thank you for getting it to me." He paused, placed the letter near the flame again, and read it once more before turning to Van Allen. "Do you know a Martin Ramsey, Philip Van Horne, or Moses Ward?"

"Yes, indeed. I know one of them," said Van Allen, his eyes widening with worry. "Van Horne is my farm manager. In fact, he asked me today if he could help with kitchen duty tomorrow. He's never asked that before. I thought he was just being helpful."

Gibbs, his face grim, turned to Van Allen and demanded, "Where can we find Van Horne?"

John grinned. Gibbs, in his role, would always be protecting.

"Probably in the barn," Van Allen answered. "Oh my." He put his large hand to his mouth.

Gibbs grabbed his pistol and darted out of the room.

The general turned to the boys. "Van Horne will be secured, I believe. As for the other two, they will not get within a mile of me now that we know their names." He nodded politely. "Thank you again. Tomorrow's breakfast or lunch might have been deadly." He placed the letter on the desk.

"Happy to have helped, sir," John said.

"Aren't you going to read the real letter too? Not just the secret message," asked Ambrose.

Washington remained serious. "No," he said. "It's a fake. A love letter from a certain—" he glanced down. "Mary Thomas." Washington raised his eyebrows as he skimmed the page. "Mary is quite exuberant in her affections."

The boys looked at one another and John stifled a laugh.

"My bride, Martha, is in Virginia. She'd have me hanged if I really were getting love letters." Washington sat back down at his desk and pulled a quill from his pot of ink.

"Mission accomplished," whispered John to Ambrose. "Dad will be proud." *If he's still alive.*

With a long sigh, Ambrose nodded. But then a mischievous glint appeared in his eye, and Ambrose walked over to a fruit bowl on the sideboard and picked up several peaches. Before John could stop him, Ambrose had them in the air, circling magically.

"General, what would you get if you crossed a patriot with a small curly-haired dog?" Peaches flew in a circle around Ambrose. "Yankee Poodle!"

George Washington looked up. John watched the general for laugher or a smile. None came.

Ambrose snatched another peach from the table and inserted it into his juggling routine. Now four peaches tumbled through his hands. "Okay, what did one flag say to the other?"

Mr. Van Allen asked, "What?"

"Nothing. It just waved."

The general's face remained blank.

John shook his head and hoped his cheeks weren't turning as red as they felt. Why did his brother embarrass him so?

"How about — "

John plucked one of the circling peaches from the air. "How about we stop this nonsense?" Several peaches dropped to the ground and the one highest above Ambrose fell on top of his head. Peach juice ran down Ambrose's cheek.

At that, Washington did laugh. But then he cleared his throat and his face regained its serious expression. "I have some letter writing of my own to complete here."

John pulled at his brother's sleeve. "No problem, sir. We understand."

"What are your names?"

"John Clark." John smiled. "Patriot John Clark."

Ambrose looked the general firmly in the eye. "Ambrose. Same last name. But you knew that," he acknowledged.

"And your father?"

"Lamberton Clark, sir," John said with a nod.

"It's a pleasure to know you," said General Washington. "I've met hundreds of young men since the start of the war. But I will not soon forget you two. You were obviously the right patriots for this job."

John's heart leapt.

They had just turned to walk out when Ambrose spun back around. "Sir, there's something we need to tell you." His voice was low. General Washington looked up and raised his eyebrows.

"The horses we rode in on ... um ... they're not ours."

John had nearly forgotten. He tugged at his ear and adjusted his feet.

"We stole them from the Connecticut Militia. But only because we had to," Ambrose added quickly, "to finish the mission."

John nodded. "We're sorry. We'll never do it again."

"Unless you have to," said the general. Both boys looked up in surprise. "In battle, we often do things we normally would never do. So much is needed for victory."

John nodded. *You've got that right.*

The general walked from behind his desk and placed one hand on John's shoulder and the other on Ambrose's. "And when we face our fears and doubts, we become better men."

Ambrose bowed his head. "I promised we'd get them back to the Connecticut militia soldiers they belong to."

"I understand what you boys did was for our cause." Washington squeezed John's shoulder. "I will write you a letter so that when you return home you will not be hanged as horse thieves."

The knot in John's stomach relaxed.

"Thank you," the twins answered.

"You must now excuse me. I have to get back to my work." Washington addressed Mr. Van Allen. "Please ensure these two patriots receive some warm food, water, and dry clothes." A pause. "Have our medic attend to their wounds. I will meet with them again tomorrow. They are welcome to sleep here tonight by a warm fire. Tell my men they are to receive the respect you'd give to one of our officers."

Ambrose nudged John with his elbow and grinned.

Washington sat down and picked up his quill, while the Dutchman escorted the boys out of the room.

As they walked down a few stairs toward the kitchen, John glanced out the window and spotted several men running frantically about the house and barn as if searching for someone or something. Major Gibbs stood near the barn, spinning to look in every direction. As John paused to take in the scene, he spotted a man crouched behind a

wagon not too far from the window. It must be Van Horne! As another wagon rode by, Van Horne darted inside the covered rear section. No one else appeared to have seen him. John gasped and his eyes widened. Dashing to and out the back door, he called out, "Major Gibbs! Major Gibbs!" John waved to the major and pointed at the wagon riding away from the house. "He's in the wagon! Over there!"

The major whistled and several of his men mounted horses and galloped toward the escaping traitor. John watched as the men shouted to the driver who halted the vehicle. The Continental soldiers drew their weapons, and one dismounted and pulled back the covering, revealing a shaken Van Horne. The soldiers immediately roped his hands and dragged him back toward the major.

Ambrose was quickly by John's side. "Not bad, brother. Nice job." He slapped John on the back. "What would these guys do without us?"

CHAPTER 18

FOR LIBERTY & SACRED HONOR

A rooster's crow woke the boys from their good night's slumber. Outside, the sky was hazy. Wagon wheels creaked and horses whinnied. The soldiers had been awake for several hours. Wincing from his bruised ribs, John stood up from his bedroll in front the fire in a room upstairs and began gathering his belongings. The night before he and his brother had eaten like gluttons, feasting on corn cakes, biscuits, carrots, and fresh milk. John's stomach rumbled like an artillery cart rolling over a bumpy road. He wondered what they would get for breakfast.

"You smell much better in those clean clothes," said Ambrose. "Face is still a mess, though."

John gently touched the white bandage on his head.

"You're just jealous because I got the general to laugh and you didn't. I can't wait to tell Sophie about that."

"Go ahead," Ambrose huffed. "It won't matter."

"If you say so." John looked out the window at the gray morning.

In minutes, they were in the kitchen, where Mr. Van Allen's wife fixed them scrambled eggs. John and Ambrose devoured them with bread, jam, and milk.

"Boys." As if he had been waiting for them to finish eating, General Washington appeared in the doorway. He was dressed in his military uniform and held a cup of tea. "Our current situation has a dark and gloomy aspect." He gestured to the window. Rain had begun to fall once more. "However, we should never despair. We've faced hard times before ... and things changed for the better, so I trust it will again. We will do whatever it takes to succeed." He looked at the boys seriously. "I want you both to promise me you will always trust Providence and fight for the cause of liberty and our sacred honor."

"We will," said John and Ambrose.

Major Gibbs entered and saluted. "Excuse me, sir. I received word that a Private Joshua Carpenter — from the Connecticut Militia — has just entered our area with two wounded prisoners of war." He smiled at the boys. "It seems they were captured yesterday with the assistance of twin boys. I will ensure proper action be taken with both of them."

"Thank you, Major," said Washington. He nodded approvingly at the twins.

John nudged his brother. "I hope they get what they deserve," he whispered.

"Sir, one of the horses we borrowed belongs to Private Carpenter," Ambrose said. "Could you please see to it that he gets it back?"

"I will take care of that myself," said Major Gibbs.

Washington cleared his throat. "Boys, we have a new mission for you. For which we will supply you with two new horses. I will be back shortly with your letter and details. Wait for me outside."

Surprised, the boys took the last bites of their bread and stood.

"What could he possibly want us to do?" John asked as they stepped outside onto the porch.

Ambrose's grin grew wider. "I don't know, but I bet it will be amazing!"

John spotted George and Thunder tied to a fence under the grist mill's overhang. "There's George."

Seeing the animals, Ambrose dodged out into the drizzling rain. John followed, splashing through muddy puddles. Under the shelter, both horses looked well-fed and rested. Ambrose ran a hand gently down George's neck.

"Hey, big fella. I . . . just came by to thank you." The steed nudged Ambrose with his nose. "You did a great job getting us here. I know your name is Buttercup, but if anyone asks . . . you tell them it's George." Ambrose stroked the velvety fur just above the horse's nostrils. "And your last name is Washington. Your first name is not King. You got that?"

George whickered.

"Or you can go by George Buttercup. That's got a nice sound to it." Ambrose nestled his head beside George's. "Be as good for Joshua as you were for me. Maybe we'll meet again someday."

John turned to his own horse. "Good-bye, Thunder," he said. He placed his head gently against the horse's neck.

A voice called from behind. "You guys were telling the truth after all!" Joshua walked briskly toward them. "You weren't planning on taking Thunder again, were you?"

"No. Of course not," John said, pleased to see him. "Actually, we were just saying good-bye."

Joshua laughed. "I was just kidding." He stepped into a deep puddle and grimaced. "I'm meeting with some of the officers here and then I'll be heading back to Connecticut tomorrow or the next day. Depending on what the weather does and when they break camp. I just wanted you to know that I'm glad we're all on the same side." He extended his hand and John shook it, followed by Ambrose.

"I'm just glad you believed us," John said.

"Make that two of us," added Ambrose.

"Express riders! Report for duty!" It was Major Gibbs. He appeared at the back door of the house with General Washington.

John turned to Joshua, who was staring at the general with a look of awe. "We have to go." Joshua nodded and John ran to the general with Ambrose at his side.

"What's our mission, General?" Ambrose asked.

"Your mission is … to go home. And report back to me via a continental courier on the condition of your father. Here's some money as well. Enough to buy food, drink, and anything else you may need to get you back to Connecticut." Washington extended his hand and provided the boys with Continental dollars. "And you may keep your new horses. Your reward for all you've done for your country and for protecting my life."

John shut his mouth when he realized it had fallen open. "Thank you, sir," he said, when he had found his voice.

Major Gibbs gestured and a soldier brought forward two horses.

"Mares?" John said.

"These gals will make good time," the major replied.

"It's okay. The ladies like me," Ambrose said.

John shook his head.

"Yours is Muffin and that's Sweetcake," replied the major.

"How come everyone in the military uses food for horse names?" Ambrose laughed.

"Our horses are as dear to us as food," said the major as he presented them with their muskets.

"I only have one pardon letter for my two horse thieves," said the General. "Who gets it?"

John gave his brother a confident look. "Give it to him," he said. "Here, Ambrose, you take Dad's musket. I had it last time. It's your turn."

Washington waited as Ambrose took the letter, removed

the plug from the musket's stock, and carefully placed it inside. "I trust in God, and that under his Providence, you will be well," Washington said. "And be watchful, boys. I may call for you to help me again someday."

John mounted his horse and patted her affectionately. "How will you know how to find us?"

"You forget," said General Washington, with a salute. "I have spies everywhere."

Proudly, John saluted in return, and Ambrose did the same. John nodded thanks to Major Gibbs and took a last long look at General Washington. The general was an even greater man than he had expected.

Finally, John turned his mare and drank in the beauty of the Van Allen property. He liked New Jersey. The valley was magnificent. A river ran below majestic green hills. John watched as Continental Army soldiers loaded crates onto covered wagons. The smell of hotcakes feeding thousands of Washington's men wafted through the air.

"By the way, I just remembered," John turned to his brother. "We have to get that rowboat we borrowed back to its owner."

"If it's still there, I'll gladly help you do so, brother." Ambrose turned his mare, and together they thundered down the road.

CHAPTER 19

WE DID IT

John kicked his mare in the side, forcing a canter as his family's home came into view. Ambrose rode swiftly beside him. John imagined that his twin's stomach was as twisted as his own. What — who — would greet them there?

Please, God, let Father be home and well.

Arriving at the front door, John jumped off Sweetcake, tied her to a post, threw open the door, and ran inside. Ambrose caught up in the hallway and pushed him out of the way.

"Dad! Mom!" both boys bellowed. "Dad! Are you all right?!"

Silence answered. John gave Ambrose a worried look.

Their eldest brother, Berty, approached from the dining room. He was grinning ear to ear. "Hey Fifer ... John."

"You're here?" John said.

"Mom sent for me when dad came home."

"Where is he?" Ambrose asked, impatiently.

171

"In his room."

John rushed through the kitchen and headed upstairs into his parent's bedroom. His father was resting in his parents' big four-poster bed. John paused briefly in the doorway and watched as the surprise registered in this father's eyes. Then he leaped onto the bed. In a moment, he felt Ambrose join the embrace as their father's arms encircled them.

A tear slid down John's cheek. His father was a great man. And John was hopefully on his way to being as courageous as him someday. It was a moment before John could make himself pull back. He looked into his father's eyes. "Are you all right?"

His father smiled. "I'm going to be fine. I just need to rest."

"Thank God," the twins said simultaneously.

"We did it, Dad," said John. "We did it."

A warm smile appeared on his father's face. "I knew you would." He sighed as he hugged his sons tightly.

Ambrose grabbed his father's hand. "Dad … General Washington is amazing."

"I'm so proud of you both," Lamberton said. "Thank God you're home safe." He looked them lovingly in the eyes. "Thank you for finishing what I couldn't."

John smiled.

Before anyone could say another word their father pulled out a fife from the bedside table and showed it to Ambrose. "I lost yours. Sorry. I had Samuel get you a new one."

Ambrose graciously accepted the fife from his father. He examined it and placed the instrument to his lips. The first few meters of a piping song filled the little room. "I love it," Ambrose blurted. "Thank you."

And now, all three of the twins' brothers crowded into the room, jostling for position, Enoch, Samuel, even Berty, followed by the boys' mother. "Thank God! You're all right!" Sarah Clark ran to her sons and wrapped them in her arms. Pulling back, she touched John's cheek. "Your face."

"Oh, it's nothing." He waved his hand.

Ambrose's smile grew wider. "Well, at least with that scar, now everyone will be certain of one thing."

"What's that?" asked their father.

"Now I'm definitely better looking than he is."

Everyone laughed.

"So tell us about your trip," Enoch said.

John and Ambrose looked at each other. "You're not going to believe what we did," they said in unison. John smiled at his brother.

As Ambrose started to tell their story, John knew what they did would have to remain a secret, to protect what their father was doing to serve the colonies, and they'd never be able to share what had happened outside this room again. He had a letter from George Washington in his satchel in case anyone accused them of being horse thieves, but he hoped he'd never have to use it. He wanted to keep the paper with Washington's signature as a remembrance of the man he felt he could now call a friend. John shook his head as Ambrose got to the part about entertaining the troops by juggling. Maybe someday in the future he'd tell his kids about what they had done. And if the patriots won the war, they would all be living in freedom.

Yeah, then it would all be worth it.

NOTE FROM
THE STORYTELLERS

The Culper spy ring actually began operating in the summer of 1778. It was established at the request of General George Washington who desperately needed reliable information about the activities and plans of the commanding officers of the British Army and Navy who were headquartered on New York Island.

Major Benjamin Talmadge was given the assignment, and he organized a small group of patriots who lived among those who were loyal to the British cause. It was a very dangerous mission since discovery meant certain death.

When information was gathered, it was sent overland by a courier as a written or coded message. The rider left from New York to a point on the Long Island shore (usually in the area of Setauket). Another courier then carried it by boat across Long Island Sound to Connecticut. From there, couriers would ride to the point of Washington's current headquarters. It took days or weeks for all of this to happen, and often the information was too old to be useful, so speed was of the essence.

Without these courageous patriots the outcome of the war might have cost us our quest for freedom.

ACKNOWLEDGEMENTS

Nothing great happens alone, and my father and I would especially like to thank the special editors who helped make our story and words sing. We are grateful for the talents of Mary Hassinger, Leslie Peterson, and Britta Eastburg from HarperCollins Christian Publishing/Zondervan. And this book would not have happened were it not for Kim Childress, formerly of Zondervan, who believed in the story from the start and served as our biggest fan and champion. Thank you all for loving our story and characters as much as we do.

DISCUSSION QUESTIONS

1. Why did the colonists call themselves patriots?

2. Why did the British royalty, Redcoats, or those loyal to King George see patriots as traitors?

3. If you were given John and Ambrose's mission, would you have accepted it? Why or why not?

4. What role did fear or extreme concern play in John's life? What are some things that make you feel that way?

5. Why did George Washington need a spy ring?

6. Why did the British military leadership need spies?

7. Ambrose had a talent for juggling (among many other things). John was an expert marksman and snare builder. What are your talents? How can you use them for a fulfilled life?

8. Ambrose said, "And so I want you all to keep your eyes on liberty, and if you do, we all shall have it." What do you think he meant by that? Explain your thinking.

9. When John's horse and gun were stolen, he didn't give up. Have you ever been in a situation when you had a "never quit" attitude? Write about it.

10. What freedoms are worth dying for?

11. Why is freedom not free?

12. Why is loyalty an important virtue? How can you show that you are loyal to a person or organization?

13. Define bravery. When did John display bravery? When did Ambrose show he was braver? When have you displayed bravery in your life?

14. In the story, John appreciated Ambrose's "smarts." Define wisdom. When did Ambrose show wisdom? John? Why is wisdom important to have?

15. John thought about what made his dad special, and part of that was that he did the right thing — even in difficult circumstances. Is that what you want too? How can you know what the right thing to do is?

16. What were some of the hardships and challenges of the continental soldiers and how did these affect them?

17. In the story and in real life, George Washington said, "Things at present have a dark and gloomy aspect. However, we should never despair. Our situation before has been unpromising ... and has changed for the better, so I trust it will again. We will put forth new exertions and proportion our efforts to the urgency of the times." Why is it important to keep hope alive when bad things happen? What does Washington's last sentence in the quote mean?

18. Although Ambrose and John are twins, they have different personalities. Describe how they are similar and how they are different and explain why you think this.

19. How has John and Ambrose's relationship changed over time and why do you think this has happened?

20. How has your life been impacted by the outcome of the American Revolution and other peoples' sacrifices as illustrated in this novel?

Historical Characters

JOHN BURGOYNE, General
(24 February 1722 — 4 August 1792)

John Burgoyne was a British army officer, politician, and playwright. Appointed to command a force designated to capture Albany and end the rebellion, General Burgoyne advanced south from Canada, but soon found himself surrounded and outnumbered by American forces. He fought two battles at Saratoga, but was forced to surrender his army of 5,000 men to the American troops on October 17, 1777.

CHARLES CORNWALLIS, General
(31 December 1738 — 5 October 1805)

General Charles Cornwallis was one of the leading British generals in the American War of Independence. He surrendered in 1781 to a combined American and French force at the Siege of Yorktown, which ended significant hostilities in North America.

THOMAS GAGE, General
(1720 — 2 April 1787)

Thomas Gage fought in the French and Indian War, where he served alongside future opponent George Washington. From 1763 to 1775, Gage was commander-in-chief of the British forces in North America. In 1774, he served as the military governor of the Province of Massachusetts Bay where he attempted to implement the Intolerable Acts, which punished Massachusetts for the Boston Tea Party. His attempts to seize Patriot military stores sparked the Battles of Lexington and Concord, beginning the American War of Independence. After the Battle of Bunker Hill in 1775, General William Howe replaced him, and Gage returned to Britain.

CALEB GIBBS
(1748 — 1818)

Caleb Gibbs was a captain in the Fourteenth Massachusetts Regiment. In 1776, General Washington picked Gibbs to command his newly established personal guard, officially known as the "Commander-in-Chief's Guard," and unofficially called the "Life Guards." It was a unique position. Gibbs was considered a member of General Washington's family, but he was also an army officer with combat command. In addition to protecting the Commander-in-Chief and the headquarters, Gibbs was responsible for selecting defensible quarters for General Washington and his staff when the army was on the move.

NATHAN HALE
(June 6, 1755 — September 22, 1776)

Hale was a young but passionate soldier for the Continental Army. When he was twenty-one, Hale volunteered for an intelligence-gathering mission in New York City, but the British captured him. He is best remembered for his last words before being hanged: "I only regret that I have but one life to give for my country."

HENDRIK VAN ALLEN (or VanAulen)

Hendrik Van Allen built and owned a Dutch Colonial farmhouse located in what is now Oakland, New Jersey. General George Washington used this home and its surrounding 200 acres of farmland as his headquarters July 14–15, 1777, when he moved his troops over "extremely deep and miry roads" from Morristown, New Jersey to Smith's Clove, New York. The house is on Ramapo Valley Road, which was a key military highway for troops and supply units during the Revolutionary War.

GLOSSARY

Culper Spy Ring British forces occupied New York in August 1776, and the city remained a British stronghold and a major naval base for the rest of the Revolutionary War. Though getting information from New York about British troop movements and other plans was critical to General George Washington, there was simply no reliable intelligence network that existed on the Patriot side. But that changed in 1778 when a young cavalry officer named Benjamin Tallmadge established a small group of trustworthy men and women from his hometown of Setauket, Long Island. Known as the Culper Spy Ring after the aliases of its main members, Samuel Culper, Sr. and Samuel Culper, Jr., Tallmadge's network became the most effective of any intelligence-gathering operation on either side during the Revolutionary War.

Kings Ferry The Kings Ferry was a major crossing point on the North (Hudson) River during the time of the Revolutionary War. It was located several miles south of the fort at West Point and connected Verplanck's Point on the east side of the Hudson with Stony Point on the west side. Since the British controlled New York City for most of the war, Kings Ferry was the southernmost crossing point that Americans could safely use to transport personnel and supplies. It was also an important communication line between the north and the south, which made Kings Ferry a strategic target for the British.

Lobsterback A slang term used by Americans for British soldiers because the red coats worn by the British resembled the red shells of cooked lobsters.

Loyalists American colonists who remained loyal to Great Britain during the American Revolutionary War; they were also called Tories, Royalists, or King's Men. They were opposed by the Patriots, those who supported the revolution. When their cause was defeated, about twenty percent of the Loyalists fled to other parts of the British Empire, many to Ontario and New Brunswick, Canada. It has been estimated that between fifteen and twenty percent of the European-American population of the colonies were Loyalists.

Musket A muzzle-loaded, smooth bore long gun, fired from the shoulder. Muskets were designed for use by infantry and included a bayonet.

North River The North River was also referred to as the Hudson River on some maps in the eighteenth century. It is commonly called the Hudson River today.

Redcoat A British soldier so named because of the red color of their uniform jacket.

Skiff A boat small enough for rowing or sailing by one person, if necessary.

The Sons of Liberty A political group made up of American patriots that originated in the pre-independence colonies. The group was formed to protect the rights of the colonists from the British government after 1766. They are best known for the Boston Tea Party in 1773, which led to the Intolerable Acts (an intense crackdown by the British government). The Patriots' counter-mobilization to these Acts led directly to the American Revolutionary War in 1775.

Tory See **Loyalists**

West Point West Point, in the state of New York, was a fortified site during the Revolutionary War. Founded by one of the best military engineers of the time, Polish General Tadeusz Koœciuszko, the site was strategically chosen for the abnormal S-curve in the Hudson River. West Point was manned by a small garrison of Continental soldiers through the entirety of the war. A great iron chain was stretched across the Hudson at this point in order to impede British Navy vessels, but it was never tested by the British. The site consisted of multiple fortifications, including Fort Putnam, which is still preserved in a Revolutionary-period design.

Letters by General George Washington

Written at the Van Aulen's home

Head Quarters, at Van Aulen's, July 14, 1777.
Parole — . Countersigns — .

Each Major General will order the guards necessary for the security of his own division.

The Quarter Master General with his deputies will mark out the ground for the encampment of each division to morrow — And as the army will arrive on its ground early in the day; as soon as the Men are settled in their quarters, the Officers are critically to inspect their arms and accoutrements, and have them put in the best order possible — The Commander in Chief was surprised today to see the bad condition of many arms they being not only unfit for fire, but very rusty, which latter defect it is certainly in the power of every man to prevent, and the neglect of it must arise from an inexcusable inattention of the officers.

The tents are to be struck at gun-firing tomorrow morning (which will be at the usual time) and the whole army got ready to march. At five o'clock one field piece is to be fired; and then the march is to begin; and as the baggage of each brigade will join its brigade to night, 'tis to follow close after it tomorrow. The whole army to march of from the left, in half platoons, the brigades following each other in the order observed this day, saving that the baggage (as before directed) will immediately follow the brigade to which it belongs — As the distance is not great, no part of the army is to halt 'till it arrives at the ground for encamping.

If it should rain tomorrow morning, the army is to remain in its present encampment.

On a *march* neither officer, nor soldier, is to pay a salute, or pull of the hat to the Commander in Chief, or other officer passing by.

Van Aulens, 8 Miles from Pompton Plains, July 14, 1777

To THE PRESIDENT OF CONGRESS

Sir: I arrived here this afternoon with the Army, after a very fatiguing March, owing to the Roads which have become extremely deep and miry from the late Rains. I intend to proceed in the Morning towards the North River, if the Weather permits; At present it is cloudy and heavy and there is an Appearance of more Rain.

By the Express, who will deliver this, I just now reced. a Letter from Genl. Schuyler, advising for the first time, that General St Clair is not in the Hands of the Enemy. As the Express has a large Packet for Congress from General Schuyler, I presume they will be informed of all the Intelligence he was possessed of respecting our Affairs in his department, and therefore I shall not trouble them with a Copy of his Letter to myself upon the Subject. I should be happy if they had a more agreeable aspect than they seem to have. I am &ca.

CHAPTER 1

GLASTONBURY, CONNECTICUT
APRIL, 1778

Ambrose Clark felt the cold, sharp blade of a bayonet on the back of his neck. "Both of you, be quiet," a voice hissed in his ear. "Don't move a muscle."

Ambrose froze, his heart pounding. His twin brother John had turned and was looking at the man behind Ambrose, his mouth open slightly in shock. Beyond him, in the darkness, Ambrose could make out a small room stacked high with wooden kegs.

"Don't say a word either." The owner of the bayonet grabbed Ambrose's upper arm and shifted the blade to the side of his neck. Not hard enough to slice a layer of skin, but hard enough to send a message that he was quite serious.

Ambrose's mind raced. Was this man friend or foe? He knew John was wondering the exact same thing. *Don't do anything stupid John … like attack this guy. I like my neck. And I like my blood inside my body where it belongs.* The blade had been placed directly over Ambrose's jugular vein. With one quick slice, Ambrose could be dead.

"Don't even think about doing anything rash to help your comrade here." The man did not speak loudly, but Ambrose did not doubt the seriousness of his threats. "If my blade doesn't kill, it could easily cripple." The man's voice was gruff and deep belonging to someone older and seasoned in combat.

Ambrose looked at John, who nodded slowly at the man. How did they not hear this man get behind them? The feat seemed impossible to Ambrose. His senses had been on high alert for the past fifteen minutes as they approached the dark buildings of the Stocking grist mill and gunpowder factory. He had only walked ten feet inside the building when he was met by that voice and blade. Had he been hiding in the dark somewhere inside or outside? How did he move so quietly with not even the wooden floor beneath him creaking? More than anything Ambrose wanted to tell the man who they were and why they were there. But he had told them not to speak. His eyes drifted slowly to John who matched his steady look. Through the shadows and over his twin's shoulder he could barely make out the image of large wood and iron machinery. Ambrose took a chance and opened his mouth to speak.

"We—" The blade stung as it pressed harder into his neck, and he quickly swallowed the rest of his sentence. Ambrose felt beads of sweat run down his forehead and the slope of his nose. His tan cotton shirt dampened with perspiration. If only their brother Berty were inside with them.

"I said don't make a sound," the man hissed. "Now, when I tell you to move I want you both to walk slowly to the door you just used to get it here. Remember, this is a gunpowder factory. Don't even think about using that pistol you have tucked in your pants, young man," he said to John. "One false move with that and we could all meet our Maker in an instant. Now, move slowly and quietly." A hand waved in Ambrose's peripheral vision, and John started walking. Then Ambrose felt a nudge in his lower back.

Ambrose slowly turned and followed his brother toward the door. Of all the doors to enter this place they had to choose the one guarded by a watchman with Indian-like skills and a sharp bayonet—who was obviously not afraid to use it first and ask questions later. They had no choice but to follow his commands. If only Ambrose had his knife. Then he could show this guy what a super sharp blade looked like. If there was one skill Ambrose had greater than most it was his ability to strike the smallest target with his knife. The ability had won him bets of skill with men twice his size and age. But it was no good wishing for it now. Ambrose stepped carefully so no sudden movements or tripping would make the blade on his neck accidentally draw blood. The floor under his feet creaked. Why hadn't they heard it when the man snuck across the boards behind them?

John slowly turned his head. His face reflected his alarm.

Ambrose exited the building behind John and stepped

into the dim light of a half moon. He knew his brother felt helpless. The feel of smooth dirt was under his feet as he took a few steps forward. Large rocks trimmed garden beds that looked like they wanted to bloom. Ambrose listened to the sound of Roaring Brook trickling beside them. The large wheel that had operated the gristmill stood still, deactivated during nonworking hours. The water running over the rocks sounded like tiny voices calling to him. If only he could speak too.

Down the road, Berty Clark held the reins of the three horses belonging to him and his two younger brothers. What was taking them so long? All they had to do was find George Stocking, wake him up, and deliver the message from Colonel Sherburne. He hoped they weren't just being shy about waking someone up. *Kids.* You give them the freedom to do something on their own and they screw it up. But Berty decided to be patient a little while longer. Perhaps Stocking was not at home. He'd give them fifteen more minutes. If they weren't back by then, he'd wake everybody up and embarrass the twins at the same time.